Nancy Drew®
in
The Phantom of Pine Hill

This Armada book belongs to:

Nancy Drew Mystery Stories® in Armada

For contractual reasons, Armada has been obliged to publish from No. 51 onwards before publishing Nos. 37–50. These missing numbers will be published as soon as possible.

Nancy Drew Mystery Stories®

The Phantom of Pine Hill

Carolyn Keene

Armada

First published in the U.K. in 1973 by
William Collins Sons & Co. Ltd, London and Glasgow
First published in Armada in 1981 by
Fontana Paperbacks,
8 Grafton Street, London W1X 3LA

This impression 1986

Armada is an imprint of
Fontana Paperbacks, part of
the Collins Publishing Group

Printed in Great Britain by
William Collins Sons & Co. Ltd, Glasgow

CONTENTS

"It's the phantom again!" exclaimed Mrs Holman

·1·

Phantom Thefts

NANCY DREW stared incredulously at the motel clerk. "But I made reservations!"

The man shrugged. "Sorry. No vacancy. We're jammed with visitors for Emerson University's June Week."

The two girls with Nancy looked despairingly at their attractive, titian-haired friend. One, George Fayne, dark-haired and boyish, declared, "The motel can't get away with this!"

Blonde, pretty Bess Marvin, George's cousin, asked in a worried tone, "What will we do, Nancy?"

"Here comes our answer—Ned Nickerson!"

A handsome, athletic young man was striding towards them, grinning broadly. He and two fraternity brothers had invited the girls for the long weekend. After greeting Ned, Nancy told him about their reservation problem.

"I'll find rooms for you," Ned assured the girls, "if Nancy wants to solve a mystery while she's here."

"Of course I do!" she exclaimed.

Ned went to a foyer phone booth and dialled a number. After a few minutes' conversation he rejoined the girls, his eyes twinkling.

"I called the uncle of one of our young professors. He lives a short distance out of town in a fine old house on Pine Hill—it's a big place with grounds that run down to the river. He's an elderly bachelor and has a housekeeper."

"Yes. Go on," Nancy urged.

"His name is John Rorick, but everyone calls him Uncle John. He likes young people and we fellows go there often."

Bess spoke up. "We're to stay at his house?"

"Yes. Uncle John was eager to have you girls as guests when I told him Nancy is an amateur detective with two fine assistants. Queer things have been happening out there lately."

Bess looked concerned. "Do you mean we may be getting into something dangerous? Dave invited me up here to have fun."

"That's why Burt asked me," said George. "But what's the mystery?"

Ned whispered, "All you have to do is catch the phantom of Pine Hill!"

"Catch the what?" Bess cried out. "A spook?"

"Uncle John will tell you all about the phantom. I'll phone Burt and Dave and tell them of the change in plans, then drive you to Pine Hill."

The girls' luggage was put back in Nancy's convertible and the group piled in, with Ned at the wheel. They drove through the pretty, tree-shaded little university town which lay at the end of a cove on a tributary of the Ohio River. Presently they turned down a side road and could see the glistening water in the distance.

"Part of the June Week entertainment will be a

pageant in the cove depicting the life of the early
settlers in the Ohio Valley," Ned told the girls. "Burt
and Dave and I will be in it."

"We'll get front-row seats," Bess said. With a
dimpled giggle, she added, "I can't wait to see you boys
in costumes. What are you going to wear?"

"That's a secret," Ned replied. "But we'll wow you!"
In a few minutes he called out, "Here we are!"

He swung left into a curving driveway and pulled up
at the front entrance of the Georgian Colonial house.
The door was opened by a tall, white-haired man with
bright blue eyes.

"Hello, Ned!" he called. "This is my lucky day. A
bevy of beautiful girl detectives!"

Ned introduced them and at once the elderly man
said, "Call me Uncle John. And welcome to my home."
He stepped aside and his housekeeper appeared. "This
is Mrs Holman, my right-hand man!"

"Thank you," the three chorused, laughing, and
Nancy added, "It is very kind of you to let us come
here. In return I'll try hard to capture your phantom."

She was thinking, "Mrs Holman is so much like our
Hannah!" Hannah Gruen, the Drews' housekeeper,
had helped Mr Drew, a busy, well-known lawyer, rear
Nancy since she was three, when her mother had died.
Nancy and Hannah were the closest of confidantes.

The trio's luggage was carried inside. From the
moment the girls stepped over the threshold, they felt at
home. The large centre hall of oak-panelled side walls
and the graceful spiral stairway, all heavily carpeted,
lent a welcoming atmosphere.

Nancy noticed, however, that the door to a room at

the left of the hallway had a stout padlock on it. Was this because of the phantom, she wondered.

Ned announced that he had to return to the university. Nancy offered to drive him there, but Ned said that the girls just had time to unpack and dress for the late-afternoon party at his fraternity house.

"I'll catch a bus at the next road. Be seeing you!"

After he had gone, Mrs Holman led the way upstairs to two adjoining rear bedrooms. They had been newly decorated with Colonial-style wallpaper, in keeping with the lovely old four-poster beds and hand-made rugs. Nancy put her bag in the smaller room, then joined her friends and the housekeeper.

"Isn't it charming!" Bess exclaimed.

Nancy hurried to a window and sighed in delight. Below was a garden of roses in a wide expanse of lawn. Behind this stood a large grove of pine trees with the sparkling water beyond.

"That's Settlers' Cove," Mrs Holman explained. "In the 1700's Mr Rorick's ancestors came down the river in a flatboat and landed here. They put their log cabin up on Pine Hill because of the lovely view. Later they built this house."

Crowning the hill across the cove were the sprawling buildings of Emerson University.

"What a marvellous sight!" Nancy exclaimed.

"It used to be beautiful at night, too, when the moon was out," said Mrs Holman. "But now—" As the housekeeper paused, Nancy thought she detected a frightened expression. The girls waited for Mrs Holman to finish the sentence. Finally, with fear in her voice, she burst out, "Now the phantom is seen flitting among the trees like a giant firefly."

"You've seen it?" Nancy asked, intrigued.

"No, but he's there all right. I'll have Mr Rorick tell you the rest. Come down when you're ready." She left the room.

Curious to hear more of the mystery, the girls quickly hung up their dresses and went downstairs. Uncle John Rorick met them at the foot of the stairway and escorted his guests through an open doorway to their left into the living-room. It ran the full depth of the house and was attractively furnished with fine eighteenth-century pieces.

Uncle John motioned his guests to tapestried chairs. Smiling, he said, "I dare say you want to learn about the phantom of Pine Hill. Apparently he wants something in my library. That's the locked room across the hall. The first time I noticed books out of place I made sure the windows were locked and put a padlock on the door. Despite these precautions, the intruder got in and has kept right on entering mysteriously!"

"It certainly sounds weird," George declared. "Do you have any clues?"

"Not one." Uncle John chuckled. "Mrs Holman declares he must be a phantom and come through our walls!"

Nancy asked Mr Rorick if he kept any money in his library. He nodded but said he had never missed any. "I must confess though," Uncle John went on, "I may have overlooked something. I'm pretty forgetful." He added, "It gives me a creepy feeling to know there's a ghostly visitor in my home."

"Oh goodness, yes," Bess agreed. "I hope I never see

this phantom. I'll lock my door and cover my head at night!"

The others laughed and Nancy said, "*I* hope I'll meet this apparition. I'm sure he's a real live person. What we must find out right now is how he enters the library."

"Right now," said Bess, "we'd better dress for the Omega Chi Epsilon party."

Reluctantly Nancy agreed. "But I'll start work on the mystery as soon as possible," she declared.

A short time later the three girls, wearing bright, colourful dresses, drove off to the campus. The fraternity house held a gay, chattering crowd of students and girls, sipping cool drinks and eating varied savouries. Nancy, Bess, and George knew many of the young people from previous parties. They were whisked from group to group by their dates.

Like Ned, Burt Eddleton and Dave Evans were athletic and played in the football team. Burt was husky and blond, while Dave, who had fair hair and green eyes, was rangy.

Presently a thin young man about twenty-five years old, with a slightly sagging jaw and wearing an ill-fitting waiter's coat, came towards the group. He was carrying a tray of lemonade on the palm of one hand, and grinning in a rather silly fashion at the guests. As he reached Nancy the glasses suddenly slid. The waiter tried to save them, but the next moment they showered their contents on to Nancy, then crashed to the floor.

Ned said angrily, "Why don't you watch what you're doing, Fred!"

"I'm sorry," the young man mumbled. He began to gather up the broken glass.

Nancy looked in dismay at her yellow dress, the front now stained and wet. "I'll have to go home and change," she told Ned.

At once he offered to drive her to Pine Hill. When they reached the house, Uncle John and Mrs Holman met them and were annoyed on hearing of the accident.

"Fred Jenkins did it," Ned explained. "He works for you sometimes, doesn't he?"

"Yes," the housekeeper replied. "Fred's clumsy here, too, but I've grown used to him. Can I help you, Nancy?"

"Oh no. Thank you, anyway." She hurried up the stairway, took off her dress, and quickly changed. "I think I'll wear my pearl necklace," Nancy decided, and reached into the pocket of her suitcase for the box. She opened it, then gasped.

The pearl necklace was gone!

Nancy closed her eyes for a moment, refusing to believe the truth. A thought instantly came to her. Had the phantom stolen her jewellery?

She returned the empty box, closed the bag, and slowly went downstairs. Nancy hated to tell Mr Rorick what had happened but felt it her duty to do so in view of the other mysterious happenings at the house. Uncle John, Mrs Holman, and Ned were astounded and immediately Mr Rorick said he would pay for a new necklace.

"That won't be necessary because Dad insured it," Nancy said. "But don't you think the police should be notified?"

"I suppose so. I'll attend to that. You run back to your party."

After Nancy had written out a description of the necklace, she and Ned drove away. He said sympathetically, "You've had a lot more excitement today than you bargained for!"

She smiled. "I loved it—except about my necklace."

After the fraternity party was over, Nancy's friends went to a country restaurant to have dinner and dance. It was midnight by the time the three girls reached home and tumbled into bed.

Nancy fell asleep immediately, but later a creaking sound awakened her.

"Someone's walking around downstairs," she thought, and in an instant was out of bed, thrusting her arms into a dressing-gown.

Nancy tiptoed into the dark hall and looked down the spiral stairway. At first there was only silence, then suddenly a door squeaked. In a few moments a shadow moved through the hall past the front windows. Then it disappeared.

The young sleuth pondered for several seconds on what to do. Should she wake up the others in the house? But this would alert the intruder, she knew, and he would escape.

"I'd better go alone and learn what I can!" Nancy decided, and cautiously started down the stairs.

· 2 ·

The Shipwreck

WHEN Nancy reached the ground floor she stood motionless. There was not a sound. Was someone watching her? She felt a chill race down her spine.

Then softly a door closed. From the location of the sound she judged it to be the outside kitchen door. Her eyes completely adjusted to the dimness, Nancy tiptoed round the staircase to an open door which led into the kitchen.

Through a window Nancy had a clear view of the moonlit garden and lawn. No one was hurrying away. Was she too late to see the intruder? And where had he gone?

Just then Nancy noticed a tiny light bobbing in the grove of pine trees, and recalled Mrs Holman's remarks about the phantom. "I wonder if he's the person who was in the house," Nancy thought, "or was it someone else?"

She overcame a desire to go outside and investigate. Although brave, the young detective tried not to take unnecessary chances. Nevertheless, from her first case, *The Secret of Shadow Ranch* to her most recent, *Nancy's Mysterious Letter*, she had often met danger while sleuthing.

17

After making sure the intruder had not unlatched the rear and front doors or any windows, Nancy went back to bed. Despite her interrupted sleep, she was the first one awake in the morning. After bathing and dressing, she hurried downstairs to examine the house for clues to the intruder.

The padlock on the library door was still in place. "He certainly couldn't have gone in there," Nancy thought. "Since he didn't pass me near the staircase, he couldn't have doubled back into the kitchen."

Only one door remained—the open one to the left at the rear of the hall. Nancy walked through the doorway into a charming, completely pine-panelled dining-room. The big mahogany table in the centre was flanked with graceful chairs. Fine old porcelain pieces lined the plate rail.

On the wall adjoining the library was a large brick fireplace with a mantelshelf. Candles in brass holders stood at each end of it.

An open door on the opposite wall led into a butler's pantry, and from there Nancy stepped into the kitchen. "I'm sure this was the phantom's route," she thought. "Maybe I scared him off!"

At that moment Mrs Holman came into the kitchen. When she heard about the intruder, the housekeeper became upset. "It's dreadful—the goings-on here! But I can't make the police believe anything's wrong. I sometimes think they suspect me!"

"Oh, I'm sure they don't," Nancy said reassuringly.

As Mrs Holman started to prepare breakfast, Nancy said she wanted to check something, then would be right back to help. She hurried to the fireplace in the dining-room, leaned down, and tapped its sooty brick walls. Nancy hoped to detect a hollow area that might mean a secret entrance to the library, but found nothing.

Just as she and Mrs Holman had breakfast ready, Mr Rorick, Bess, and George came downstairs. The elderly man was dressed for travelling and told the girls he was leaving for a class reunion at his college several hundred miles away.

He chuckled. "I expect you to have my mystery solved by the time I get back," he said.

"I hope I can," Nancy answered.

After they sat down at the table, Nancy told the others what had happened the night before. They were astounded and Uncle John remarked, "It may have been a real burglar instead of our phantom."

"I don't think so," Mrs Holman spoke up. "None of the silver is missing. I checked when I set the table."

Bess dug a spoon into her grapefruit. "I don't know which is worse—burglars or spooks. I just hope both of them leave me alone!"

When the group finished breakfast, Mr Rorick said he would give the key to the library padlock to Mrs Holman so his "girl detective force" could investigate at any time.

"Thank you," said Nancy.

"Before I go, would you be interested in hearing a little of the Rorick family history?" he asked.

"Yes, indeed. It's just possible there might be some connection between that and your phantom," Nancy suggested.

"Hmm," said Uncle John. "I never thought of that.

You may be right. Perhaps it has something to do with the lost gifts."

The girls listened intently as he went on, "When my ancestor, George Rorick, came to this country he brought a French bride with him—a young noble-woman. She kept in close touch with her family, and when her daughter Abigail was to be married, the relatives in France sent a chest of wedding gifts. But the steamship it came on had an explosion aboard and sank in the river not far from Settlers' Cove. A short time before, a letter and a key came to Abigail from her uncle in France. I still have the key hidden away. The letter is hanging on the wall. I'll get it."

He excused himself and went to the library, but returned in a minute with a framed letter. It was dated 1835, and was written in French in an old-fashioned, precise script. Many of the words were no longer in use.

Uncle John turned the frame over. Pasted on the back was an English translation. The very gracious letter said the writer's family sent felicitations and wished the bride-to-be and her husband great happiness. A chest containing presents—a wedding dress, veil, fan, slippers, and a very special gift—was being shipped on a freighter but should reach Miss Abigail Rorick in plenty of time.

"How exciting!" said Bess.

Nancy was still reading. Abigail's uncle was at the time a member of the court of Louis Phillipe. The queen herself had selected the material for the gown and veil in Paris. The beautiful fan was a gift from her.

"They must have been lovely," Nancy said softly.

George asked, "What was the family's other gift to Abigail?"

"No one knows, but I'm sure it was valuable," Uncle John answered. "The report was that when the *Lucy Belle* sank, most of those aboard and the cargo were lost. A few of the passengers and crew were saved, but probably took only some personal possessions ashore—if any. We don't know if the gifts went down or not. And in those days no one could dive deep enough to retrieve cargo. By now the lighter pieces would have shifted and been buried in mud."

"But it is possible that in recent times scuba divers may have removed the cargo," Nancy remarked.

Mr Rorick smiled. "I doubt it. The story of the *Lucy Belle* has long since been forgotten."

Nancy asked thoughtfully, "Where did the people who were saved go, Uncle John?"

"I don't know. Maybe some of the old books in my library will tell you. There are many I've never read."

Bess asked if the *Lucy Belle* had come directly from France. Mr Rorick shook his head. "The gifts were shipped across the Atlantic to Baltimore. Then they came overland by stagecoach to Pittsburgh. There they were put on the *Lucy Belle* and came up the Ohio and into this tributary. Abigail received notice of this."

Uncle John took the old letter back to the library, then went for his suitcase. Within minutes he was in his car, waving farewell and wishing the girls luck.

But there was one more delay before Nancy could start investigating the library. A young detective arrived to take Nancy's fingerprints, since she had been out the night before when he came to investigate the case of the missing necklace.

After he had gone, Mrs Holman unfastened the pad-locked door and the girls went in. Like the living-room, the library extended from the front of the house to the back.

"Oh," said Bess, "I've never seen so many books in one room. There must be thousands of them!"

Every wall was lined with shelves from floor to ceiling and filled with double rows of books. Many of the volumes looked old and fragile. A quick survey indicated a wide variety of subjects.

There were two windows on each of the outside walls, all of them securely locked. The fireplace was a duplicate of the one in the dining-room and was back to back with it.

Nancy again wondered if there were a passage between them. Then she noted the undisturbed ashes and bits of charred wood.

"If there's a secret opening," Nancy reasoned, "the phantom hasn't used it." Nevertheless, she tested the brick facing, but found no sign of a hidden entrance.

Next, Nancy studied the layout of the room. It contained a large desk which stood in the centre, several small Oriental rugs, and a safe under one front window. A long red-leather couch and matching chairs were scattered about.

"Pretty cosy place to browse," George remarked. "Well, Nancy, where do we start hunting for the phantom?"

"I suggest you begin looking through the books for a clue to why the phantom is interested in this room. Mrs

Holman, will you see if anything is missing? Bess, help me roll up these rugs. There may be a trap door underneath."

Presently the housekeeper reported that nothing was gone so far as she knew. Nancy and Bess did not discover a trap door, and relaid the rugs. Mrs Holman was about to leave the room, when George suddenly cried out:

"Wow! Guess what I've found!"

·3·

Photo Finish

As Mrs Holman, Bess, and Nancy hurried across the library, George held out an open book. In it was a sizeable heap of bills.

"My goodness!" the housekeeper exclaimed. "Did you find all that money in the book?"

George nodded. "I noticed the volume was standing upside down. When I took it out to turn it round, this is what I found."

Quickly Mrs Holman counted. "A hundred and fifty dollars!" she exclaimed.

Nancy, her eyes on the open page, noticed that the number was 150. She brought this to the attention of the others. As the money was returned and the book closed, they all read the title. It was *The Roaring Twenties*.

Nancy chuckled. "I'll bet Uncle John hides his money this way. The word *roar*—or *roaring*—may help him recall the book because of his name Rorick."

The housekeeper suggested that they check on Nancy's theory and everyone began searching. They noticed a number of books with *roar* in the title on the shelves to the left of the fireplace. "Uncle John keeps them all in this section, I'll bet," said Nancy.

"Look here!" said Bess, holding out a volume.

The title of it was *The Roaring River*, and on page 200 were ten crisp twenty-dollar bills! In a moment George came upon *The Roar of the Wilderness*. On page 50 lay a fifty-dollar bill.

There was no question now in anyone's mind but that Uncle John used this method to hide money. Had the phantom somehow found this out? And had he been removing bills?

"But," Mrs Holman said, "that still doesn't explain how he gets into this room. Well," she added, "I'll leave that to you girls and go back to my chores."

After she left, they continued their investigation and found several more books with the word *roar* in the title. The total amount of money they had uncovered was over a thousand dollars!

Bess sighed. "This is the most unique bank I've ever been in—not that I've been in many. I'm afraid my allowance and the money I've earned don't find their way to a bank account!"

"Shame on you, Cousin Bess," said George with mock severity.

A clock on Mr Rorick's desk chimed eleven. "We'd better go and dress," said Bess. "We're due at the Omega House at twelve."

"That's right," Nancy agreed. "And the crew race won't wait for us."

During the afternoon there was to be the final race of the season. Emerson would be pitted against Wellbart. Ned Nickerson was stroke for Emerson. Since each crew had already won six races, the competition was high.

Nancy padlocked the library door, returned the key, and the girls went to dress. They put on simple but attractive casual dresses, then set off in Nancy's car for the fraternity house. They found it filled with an excited crowd. Everyone was rooting for Emerson to win and the din was deafening.

Ned said to Nancy, "If I don't get out of this noise, I won't have any energy left for the race. Let's go out under the trees to eat. I'll get a couple of plates of food from the kitchen."

He led Nancy outside to a large oak some distance from the fraternity house, then went back. A few minutes later he returned with two paper plates heaped with food. Grinning, he said, "I won't dare eat much of this or I'll sink the shell!"

Nancy laughed and Ned asked, "Have you caught the spook yet?"

"I almost did," Nancy answered, and told him about the episode of the previous night.

She was about to mention the hunt in the library when a wasp landed in the midst of her food. As she jumped up to flick it away, she caught sight of Fred Jenkins standing behind the oak tree.

Ned, too, saw him. "What are you doing here?" Ned demanded.

Fred's face turned red and he stammered, "I—I was just coming to see if I could bring you anything else."

"If we want more food we'll get it," Ned told him. "You're supposed to be serving in the house. Hadn't you getter get back on the job?"

After Fred had gone, Nancy remarked, "He certainly acted guilty of eavesdropping. Since he works for Mr

Rorick, do you suppose he knows something about the mystery?"

Ned grinned. "If he didn't, he does now. Probably he heard every word you said. I only hope he won't go telling it all over town."

Glancing at his wrist watch, Ned said that it was time for him to change for the race. Then he escorted Nancy back to the fraternity house. "Remember, your seats are in the front row. I'll be listening for your cheering!"

Shortly before two o'clock the five young people found their places on the shore front below the college buildings. A band was playing a lively tune. Emerson and Wellbart banners were being waved.

Bess was chalk-white. "I'm so nervous," she said, then explained to Dave, "I always get nervous at races."

"To tell you the truth, I don't feel so calm myself," said Dave. "The Wellbart crew is mighty good."

Minutes later, the announcement of the race was made. Nancy could feel herself tensing up and held on tightly to the sides of her chair. A pistol sounded. The contestants were off!

Everyone stood up to watch the two crews. They were neck and neck as they sped across the river. Then one shell shot in front.

"Oh dear, Wellbart's ahead!" Bess said dolefully.

The words were hardly out of her mouth when the Emerson crew pulled forward. "Emerson's going to win!" cried George.

As the two shells entered the cove, the Wellbart crew caught up and rowed nearly half a boat length beyond their opponent.

"Ned! Ned! Come on!" shouted Nancy.

Emerson did catch up, and with the coxswain working his men hard, his crew pulled ahead ever so slightly. Nancy and her friends felt encouraged and screamed at the top of their voices.

Wellbart backers were equally excited. "Don't let 'em win!" cried one youth, waving a banner wildly. "Show 'em what you've got!"

The next moment the two shells were exactly even. The screaming and rooting increased.

"Oh, Ned!" Nancy cried out. "Get ahead! Get ahead!"

Both shells were nearing the finish line now. Still they looked as if they were even. The two coxswains, moving forward and backward in a frantically fast rhythm, were shouting snappy orders.

Nancy's heart was thumping madly. The excited girl was almost too choked to breathe and cry out any more. She dug her nails into the palms of her hands and never took her eyes off Ned. To herself she said, "Stroke! Stroke! You've got to win!"

Suddenly both shells slid across the finishing line. Instantly people began to call out, "Who won?"

"It's a photo finish!" Dave cried out. "We won't know for a few minutes."

A sudden hush had come over the crowd as everyone waited for the result. The heaving men in the shells sat quiet and tense, their paddles raised.

Presently the head judge stepped to the microphone. He smiled. "I know you are all eagerly awaiting the results so I will not prolong my speech except to say that personally I have never seen a better race. I congratulate every man on his good sportsmanship and fine performance. The result according to the high-speed camera shows that the winner—is Emerson University!"

"Yea! Yea!" a shout went up, then the Emerson rooters gave the college yell. The Wellbart men gave theirs, ending it with, "Emerson! EMERSON! EMERSON!"

The crew saluted with their paddles, then rowed to their boathouse.

"I've never seen anything so exciting in my life!" said Bess. "I'm exhausted!"

After a round of hugs and enthusiastic chatter, the five young people sat down to await Ned. He came in about half an hour and received excited congratulations from his friends.

"Thanks," he said. "That race sure was a tough one. To tell you the truth, I thought we had lost." He grinned. "I'm all in favour of high-speed cameras!"

After the excitement had died down, he asked Nancy if she would go out with him in a canoe. "Oh, I'd love to," she replied. "Let's visit the area where the *Lucy Belle* is supposed to have sunk."

They said goodbye to the other two couples and went to the boathouse. Nancy offered to paddle, but Ned only laughed, saying this would be an easy task after the gruelling race. He started across the large cove and then hugged the shore line on the opposite side.

"After talking with you about the *Lucy Belle* last night, Nancy, I recalled something that happened in our college library a couple of weeks ago. I noticed two men—I'm sure they didn't belong to the university—standing behind one of the stacks of books. At first I paid no attention to them, but when one of them, who had a deep, hoarse voice, mentioned 'the Rorick treasure,' I listened. Then they left."

Nancy was interested at once. "I wonder who they were. Did you see them?"

"Sorry. I didn't. But I did notice a book on the table which I'm sure they were looking at. It was a history of early Ohio River boats."

"They must have been looking up the *Lucy Belle*," said Nancy. "Ned, if you ever happen to see those men again, try to find out who they are."

Ned smiled. "At your service, Miss Detective."

She now told him about Abigail Rorick's wedding chest. "Maybe those men believe it is not lost! They might even think it was buried, and be hunting for it in the woods behind Uncle John's house! That would explain the phantom's light."

"Could be," Ned replied.

"I wish I knew more about the sinking of the *Lucy Belle*," Nancy said.

"I don't know anything about the boat, but I can tell you a few stories about the history of this area that might give you a clue. Would you like Professor Nickerson to lecture?" he asked, a twinkle in his eye.

"Please do," Nancy begged.

" 'Way back in 1807 the inhabitants of the Ohio Valley found it difficult to get cash. Silver dollars were scarce and the practice grew of dividing them into eight equal wedge-shaped pieces. These fractions got the nickname of bits and from this came the phrase "two bits," meaning one-quarter or two-eighths of a dollar!"

Nancy smiled. "I've always wondered when I hear

people mention 'two bits' where the name came from. Tell me another bit of history."

Ned said that Ohio River ports were stations for prospectors on their way to California during the Gold Rush of 1849. This was where they stocked up with provisions, including salt.

"Did you know that the first mineral product of the Ohio Valley was salt?" Ned asked. When Nancy shook her head, he went on, "As you know, salt has been an essential food for man and animal since the beginning of time. In prehistoric days salt attracted not only human inhabitants to this area, but also animals like the giant sloth, the mammoth elk, deer, and buffalo."

"That's fascinating," said Nancy. "Don't stop."

"Professor will relate one more story and that's the end of his knowledge." Nancy giggled and Ned went on, "The Indians here were frightened that the white men would take away all their territory, so they raided and burned settlements. It was not until the American Army took over that the raids were stopped, around 1794."

By this time Ned was nearing Pine Hill. Nancy happened to look up the high embankment at the woods which ran to the Rorick garden. Suddenly she caught a flash of sunlight on glass.

"Ned," she said, "somebody is watching us with binoculars! See him up there among the trees?"

Ned turned to look, resting his paddle. "You think that's your phantom?" he asked.

Nancy shrugged as they squinted into the afternoon sun, trying to see what the man looked like.

Both she and Ned had heard the sound of a motorboat

but had paid no attention. Suddenly they realized it was very close to them. The two turned and were horrified to see the craft bearing down on them.

Ned dug his paddle into the water and tried to get out of the way as Nancy shouted and waved her arms to the pilot of the motorboat. But the man, crouched low behind the wheel so that his face could not be seen, paid no attention.

A moment later he crashed into the side of the canoe. It shot out of the water and capsized, tossing Nancy and Ned overboard!

·4·

Mysterious Thumbprints

SMACK! Nancy and Ned hit the water and disappeared beneath the surface for a few seconds. Then both clawed their way to the top.

"You okay?" they asked in unison.

Each nodded but declared that they certainly had had a fright.

They swam towards the overturned canoe which was badly scraped on one side. The paddle Ned had been using was smashed and the extra one that had been in the bottom of the canoe had floated away.

"What a mess!" Ned said in disgust.

Treading water, the couple talked over what to do. Since they were close to shore, they decided to swim in and tow the canoe. Then they would climb the embankment and trek through the woods to the Rorick home for dry clothes.

"Do you think that pilot hit us on purpose?" Ned asked as he beached the canoe on the gravelly shore. "You were facing him. What did he look like?"

Nancy said she had been unable to see his face. "Maybe he was just a bad pilot," she added.

Ned shook his head doubtfully as he and Nancy began to climb the bluff. Upon reaching the woods, both

33

looked left and right for a sign of the man who had been spying on them. No one was in sight.

"That guy with the binoculars certainly took my mind off my job," Ned said ruefully. "When I first heard that motorboat I should have paddled out of the way."

Nancy said thoughtfully, "I can't figure out why that pilot didn't see us."

"Meaning that you think he meant to run us down," said Ned. "You're coming around to my point of view." He grinned.

Nancy made a wry face but did not answer. It was cool in the woods and she began to feel cold and clammy in her soaking wet clothes.

"Let's hurry!" she urged, and started off at a jog. Ned followed.

Mrs Holman answered their ring at the back door and looked at the couple aghast. "What in the world have you been doing?" she asked.

Quickly Nancy explained and the woman's face took on a worried look. At once she had a solution. "That phantom was watching in the woods and he has a confederate with a motorboat!"

"Maybe," Nancy said, shivering.

The housekeeper became solicitous. She told the young detective to go up and change. Mrs Holman herself would find some of Mr Rorick's clothes for Ned to wear. "Follow me," she directed.

As Nancy paused at her own bedroom, she said, "Mrs Holman, have you a paddle here?"

The housekeeper nodded, saying that there were several in the cellar and Ned could help himself.

"I'll walk back to the shore with you, Ned," said Nancy. "I'd like to look for clues to the person who was spying on us."

In a few minutes the two young people were ready. Nancy had put on slacks and a shirt.

She tried hard to keep from smiling as she looked at Ned. Mr Rorick certainly went in for colourful clothes! She knew that Ned would be the victim of a lot of teasing when he reached the fraternity house, so she refrained from any of her own.

The couple walked through the woods slowly, keeping their eyes alert for footprints or any other clues to the man who had been watching them, but saw none.

"If that was the phantom he has winged feet," Ned said finally, as he started down the embankment. "Be careful on your way back. I need you for the dance tonight. Burt and Dave and I will pick you girls up at seven."

After he had paddled off, Nancy studied the edge of the embankment.

"Let's see. That spy was standing over near those birches." From the water she had noticed a clump of white birch next to the pine trees which the man was using for a shield. She went to the spot and picked up his footprints. The short spaces between the small-sized shoe marks indicated that he was a slight man of medium height.

The prints led along the top of the bluff for a short distance, then went down through thick bushes to the water. Nancy guessed the man had been hiding among the brush until the couple had left the area.

"Someone must have met him in a boat, unless he

had one hidden among the bushes and Ned and I didn't see it."

The young sleuth retraced her steps up the embankment, looking for further clues. She saw nothing and with a sigh headed for the house.

The shadows were long as Nancy hurried through the woods. Suddenly she stopped short. Floating down towards her, seemingly out of nowhere, was a small white paper. As it fell almost at her feet, she looked up in the trees to see where it had come from. There was no person, bird, or animal in sight.

"I could almost believe there *is* a phantom in these woods," Nancy murmured to herself as she stooped to pick up the piece of paper.

Her eyes grew wide in astonishment. On the paper were two large, very black, well-defined thumbprints!

For several seconds Nancy did not move. There had been a few times in her life when she had been utterly confounded by some event which seemed to hold no explanation except a supernatural one. This was one of those times. But presently she shook off the mood, telling herself this was nonsense. Someone had put those prints on the paper. But where and why? And how had it come to float down to her? Were these the phantom's thumbprints?

Nancy took a handkerchief from her pocket and carefully wrapped the paper in it. Holding it in her hand, she continued to walk towards the house, hoping to find someone on the way. But there was not a sound in the grove.

When she reached the house she found Bess and George in the kitchen with Mrs Holman. The housekeeper had just finished telling them what had happened to Nancy and Ned.

George looked at Nancy. "Gosh!" she said. "We let you out of our sight for two hours and *whamo!*"

Nancy laughed. "Wait until I show you something else," she said, and opened the handkerchief.

Bess gave a little cry. "That's creepy! Where did it come from?"

Nancy told the girls and Mrs Holman. George insisted that someone was playing a trick on Nancy, but Bess and the housekeeper were worried.

"This is a bad omen, Nancy," Mrs Holman remarked. "I don't know how much more I can stand of this phantom!"

Nancy put an arm round the woman. "Please don't worry. We'll get to the bottom of this yet."

"All right," the housekeeper conceded. "I'll try to keep calm. But my dear, be careful."

After Nancy promised, George said, "Come on now, girls. Time to make ourselves beautiful!"

"This is really dress-up night," Bess remarked as they hurried to their rooms. "The dance is going to be a honey, I know. Dave was telling me about decorating the gym."

As usual, Bess had chosen a flowing dress with a full skirt, while George's choice was quite simple and fitted her boyish figure admirably. Nancy was wearing a yellow evening gown, embroidered in white with birds and flowers. It had a fitted top with an A-line skirt. She secretly hoped that Ned would like it. He had never seen it.

Nancy was a quick dresser and was ready before the

other girls. She called into their room, "See you down-stairs. I'm going to a little sleuthing while I'm waiting for you."

As she came down the stairs, Fred Jenkins walked across the hall from the living-room. He stared at her in complete astonishment and admiration.

"M-Miss Nancy, you look positively—super!" As Fred spoke he let a vase of flowers he was carrying crash to the floor. He looked down in dismay. "See what you made me do! You shouldn't be so beautiful! You take my mind off my work!"

Nancy wanted to smile. Instead, she said, "I'm terribly sorry."

Just then Mrs Holman came bustling from the kitchen. She took in the scene at a glance.

"Oh, Fred," she said angrily, "that was one of Mr Rorick's favourite vases."

Fred Jenkins said, "I couldn't help it."

"Well, don't just stand there," Mrs Holman said. "Go get the dustpan and broom and a clean cloth to wipe up this mess."

Nancy came on down the stairs and Mrs Holman beckoned her to come into the dining-room. "You mustn't mind Fred," she said. "He just can't seem to hold on to things. I keep him because it's hard to get help and he's the soul of honesty."

Nancy, recalling his standing behind the tree while she and Ned were talking, asked, "Does he know about the phantom?"

"I'm sure he doesn't," Mrs Holman replied, "or he'd never work here. He'd be too scared!" She smiled broadly and winked at Nancy.

Quietly Nancy told the housekeeper she was about to do some sleuthing. Just then Fred appeared in the doorway to report that he had swept up the broken vase, picked up the flowers, and mopped the floor. Now, he said, he must leave.

After he had gone, Nancy went to look at the wall on either side of the library door. Was one of the panels a secret entrance to the room? She stepped close to tap for a hollow sound.

· 5 ·

Two Spies

As Nancy went from panel to panel of the hall, tapping each one and listening carefully, Mrs Holman came to her side. "I've never seen a sleuth at work," she said with a smile. "Show me how to do it."

Nancy illustrated by laying her head against the wood and tapping softly with her fingers. As she finished "listening" to the woodwork on either side of the fireplace, Nancy sighed. "I'm sorry not to be able to show you what I mean. These walls are solid."

Nancy glanced at her watch. There was still plenty of time for some investigating before the girls would have to leave for the Omega House.

"Mrs Holman, would you mind unlocking the door to the library? I'd like to tap the walls there."

The housekeeper went for the key and inserted it into the padlock. As the two entered the room, Mrs Holman looked around uneasily, but nothing had been disturbed.

Nancy smiled. "Now," she said, "maybe I can show you what I mean."

After a few minutes of work, she reported there were no hollow-sounding panels.

The housekeeper frowned. "Then there's only one

answer to the phantom getting in here. He *must* be a spook and come through the walls!"

Nancy knew there was no point in contradicting Mrs Holman, but she was amazed that this intelligent person could possibly believe what she had just said. On a sudden hunch Nancy went to look at the book titled *The Roaring Twenties*. As she opened it, the young detective looked grim.

There were now only one hundred and forty dollars instead of one hundred and fifty. Moreover, the bills had been moved to page 140!

A thought which had been building up in Nancy's mind now became even more disturbing. The only person with a key to the padlock was Mrs Holman herself! Was it possible that the housekeeper had invented the story of the phantom to cover up thefts of her own?

"I just don't want to believe such a thing!" Nancy told herself. "But I'm trying to solve this mystery for Mr Rorick. I mustn't get soft-hearted and miss a clue."

Hiding her feelings, she walked out of the library. After Mrs Holman had locked it, Nancy said, "Would you do me a big favour?"

The housekeeper smiled. "I'll be glad to if it's not too difficult."

Nancy had decided to put Mrs Holman to a test of honesty. "Oh, it's a very simple request. I'd like to borrow this key for tonight. After I get home from the dance, I may want to hide in the library and watch for the phantom."

Mrs Holman looked startled. "Do you think that's safe?" she asked.

"Oh, I'll keep well hidden," Nancy replied.

Mrs Holman handed over the key. "Good luck. I'd certainly like to see this house rid of that spooky creature. He makes me so nervous!"

Nancy smiled, then started back upstairs to hide the key in her bedroom. "After we return from the dance," she thought, "I'll investigate the books with the money in them. If any more has been taken—or there's other evidence that someone has been in the room during the evening—it'll make Mrs Holman's guilt unlikely. Of course," Nancy admitted to herself, "there's the possibility that she has another key—"

Just then the telephone rang. Nancy paused for a moment on the stairway to see if the call were for her. Mrs Holman answered and almost instantly said, "Oh no! Y-yes, I'll come at once."

As the housekeeper put down the phone, Nancy asked, "Is something wrong?"

"My niece—Jill Ball—was in an accident. She's in the hospital. Her husband wants me to come to his house tonight and take care of the children. Do you think you girls will be safe here alone? Oh, I hope the phantom—"

Nancy expressed her sympathy and said the girls would be all right. Mrs Holman gave Nancy the front door key. Within a few minutes a taxi came for the housekeeper and she left.

Bess and George were ready by this time and in a few minutes the boys arrived in a big car which they had hired for the evening. They drove to the Omega House, where the dinner party was being held. Finally the couples began to leave for the university gymnasium. Nancy, Bess, George, and their escorts walked over together.

As they entered the big building, Bess gasped. "What marvellous decorations!" she exclaimed. "How in the world could you boys ever think up anything so artistic?"

Their three escorts pretended to be hurt. Dave remarked, "What makes you girls think you have a corner on the artistic market?"

The apparatus in the gym had been entirely concealed with garlands of artificial roses. The centre of the floor had been left free for dancing. Tables holding six to twelve had been arranged around four sides, with each two tables screened by latticework which was also festooned with roses.

"Your decorating committee deserves a big cheer," said Nancy. "I've never been to a dance with such pretty arrangements."

The boys grinned. "Ladies," said Burt, "on behalf of Mr Nickerson, Mr Eddleton, and myself, I thank you."

"Our achievement was nothing," Ned declared. "It was only great."

Before the laughing girls could retort, there was a roll on a drum—the official announcement that the party had started. For nearly an hour, as broiled chicken, mashed potatoes, fresh peas, salad, and ice cream and cake were served, there was continuous laughter and joking.

Finally Bess remarked, "Please don't anyone else be funny. I've laughed so much I hurt all over."

"Tell you what," said Dave, who was far from ready

to be serious, "we'll take you to the infirmary and give you some laughing gas. Then it won't hurt when someone pulls a joke."

Later, as Nancy was dancing with Ned, she told him of her early-evening sleuthing, of the missing money, and her plan to make a search when she reached home.

Ned said quickly, "I can't believe that Mrs Holman is guilty."

"I don't either," Nancy replied, "but you'll admit that I must try to find out. There is a possibility that she might even have had a confederate phone this evening to throw us off the scent."

Nancy went on to say that if the money had not been touched, she planned to spend the balance of the night hiding in the library to see if anyone entered it.

Ned looked worried. "Nancy, I don't want you to do that alone. It's too dangerous. How about letting me keep watch with you? If the phantom comes, I'll give him the old football rush!"

Nancy hesitated before answering, but finally said, "Bess and George may be hurt if I don't ask them."

"Don't worry about that," said Ned. "I'll talk to them."

The dance number ended, and as they went back to the table, Ned called Bess and George aside and explained what he proposed.

"It's a good idea," said Bess. "I'll feel safer with a man in the house. And no sleuthing for me tonight. I'm too tired."

George liked the plan, but Nancy thought she detected a gleam of mischief in her friend's eye.

"I'd better watch my step," Nancy thought. "George has some trick up her sleeve, I'm sure."

It was in the small hours of the morning that the dance ended and the six young people finally returned to the Rorick home. Bess suggested that they have a snack in the kitchen and in a short time she was scrambling eggs and making toast and a huge pot of cocoa.

When they finished eating, Dave threw out his arms and yawned. "I'm ready to call it quits. Any extra beds in this old house?"

George said quickly, "I'm afraid not, but how about the floor? That's free!"

"Gosh, but you're hospitable," said Burt. "Just for that I won't help wash the dishes."

A few minutes later Burt and Dave drove off. The others tidied the kitchen, then Bess and George went upstairs.

Nancy opened the padlock on the library door, and she and Ned went inside. Before turning on the lights, she drew the draperies close together so no one could look in to see the searchers. This done, she went for the book *The Roaring Twenties*. To her relief, the hundred and forty dollars was still on page 140.

Next, she went to the volume *The Roaring River*. A twenty-dollar bill was gone and the balance of the bills had been placed twenty pages lower. Nancy quickly picked out book after book with the word *roar* in the title. Ten dollars had been taken from each of them and the bills shifted to a page which corresponded to the remaining amount!

"The phantom has been here!" Nancy exclaimed.

Ned frowned. "I think the rest of the money should be removed from this room and put in the bank. It's certainly not safe here!"

Nancy agreed. Then Ned asked her if she had any theories as to who the phantom could be. "Surely not Mrs Holman?"

"Probably not, but to make sure she wasn't faking, I'm going to call the hospital," Nancy said.

She learned that Jill Ball was indeed a patient there. Her frantic husband was by her bedside, but the head nurse was very reassuring. Their children were being cared for by an aunt.

"That completely exonerates Mrs Holman," Nancy told Ned in relief as she came into the library and closed the door. "As far as a solution to the mystery goes, I'm right back where I started."

"Well, I guess there's no use in our staying here any longer. I'm sure the phantom won't come back again tonight."

As the couple gathered all the money and made notations on a pad of the amount taken from each book, Ned produced a theory. "Didn't it ever occur to you that Uncle John might be more than just forgetful?"

"What do you mean?" Nancy asked.

"I mean," Ned replied, "that Uncle John might be having a little fun at the expense of you girls. He probably has a duplicate key to this padlock."

The young sleuth was astounded by the remark. "Uncle John?" she said. "I can't believe it! He didn't know until you telephoned him that we were coming here. According to Mrs Holman, the mysterious happenings had been going on for a couple of weeks before that."

Ned said it was possible Uncle John was having fun at Mrs Holman's expense.

A determined look came over Nancy's face. "There's an easy way to learn if he came here tonight," she said. "Tomorrow morning I'll find a pretence for phoning Uncle John at his college reunion, and find out where he was tonight."

Nancy asked Ned to put the roll of money into his pocket. Then the lamps were turned off and the draperies opened. As Nancy pulled aside one to a rear window, she cried, "The light! See it out there in the woods!"

Ned could detect a small moving light among the trees near the river. "So that's the phantom," he remarked.

"Come on! Let's investigate!" Nancy urged.

As they hurried towards the door, they heard a low moaning sound.

"Stand back!" Ned ordered Nancy.

He whipped open the door and stepped into the hall. The next second a hood was thrown over his head and he was borne to the floor!

· 6 ·

A Revengeful Spook

WHEN Nancy heard Ned's muffled cry, she rushed into the hall. It was dimly lighted by a lamp on the first-floor hall. She could see no one but struggling Ned. Quickly she pulled the hood off him, then snapped on the switch to the ceiling light. She found herself holding a pillowcase!

She returned to Ned, who was on his feet now. Suddenly he thought of the money. He ran his hand into his trousers' pocket. The roll of bills was still there!

He said to Nancy, "Anyway, my attacker didn't intend to rob me—unless he had no time, with you arriving on the scene so soon."

Nancy was already hunting around the floor for evidence. Suddenly the young sleuth giggled as she came across a pale-blue ribbon sash. She picked it up and walked close to Ned.

"This is from Bess's robe!" she whispered. "She and George pulled this trick!"

The couple searched and found the two culprits hiding in the dining-room.

"Okay, girls," said Ned. "You just wait! When I tackle you with a pillowcase some day, it'll be full of feathers!"

48

Before locking the door to the library, Nancy looked out the back window again. The light in the woods was gone.

"I was afraid of that," she said. "George Fayne, you and Bess made me miss my chance to go after the phantom."

The two girls said they were sorry and Nancy remarked that she would keep her eyes open for another opportunity. The group went upstairs and Ned was shown into Mr Rorick's bedroom.

"Thanks. And, by the way, I'll probably leave here before you girls are up. Everyone in the pageant is due for an early-morning rehearsal."

"But where will you have breakfast?" Bess asked solicitously.

"Oh, I'll grab a bite at the fraternity house." Ned took the roll of notes from his pocket. "Nancy, I'd better leave this money with you. I think you should ask Mr Rorick's or Mrs Holman's permission to remove it from the house."

Nancy agreed. The following morning Mrs Holman returned just before breakfast. She reported her niece was out of danger and that the young woman's mother had arrived to take care of the children.

"I'm glad to hear Mrs Ball is better," Nancy said. Then she told Mrs Holman about her discovery that money was missing. The woman said she would feel better if it were in safe keeping.

"Would it be possible for you to call Uncle John at his college reunion and ask him about it?" Nancy queried.

"That's a good idea," the housekeeper agreed. "I'll do it right now before he goes out."

She hurried to the telephone in the hall. When she reached her employer, she beckoned Nancy to come and talk with Mr Rorick. Laughingly, the young detective asked if he had enjoyed himself the previous evening and he went into a long explanation of the party for the old-timers at his fraternity house. Nancy was satisfied that he was really there.

She thought, "He's definitely not the phantom."

When Nancy told him that the girls had discovered the money in the books and that it was being stolen, he became alarmed. "You must catch that phantom thief!" he said.

"I'm doing my best, but it may take a while," Nancy answered. "In the meantime, may I have your permission to put the money in a safe place—your bank for instance?"

"Suppose you take it to the college bursar."

"Fine, I'll do it right away," Nancy promised.

Twenty minutes later the three girls drove up to the administration building on the campus. Nancy found the bursar to be a very understanding man and a great friend of Mr Rorick. "I'll mark this money with John's name and keep it in the safe," he said.

Nancy thanked the bursar. She got a receipt and left his office.

As she rejoined Bess and George at the car, Nancy said, "Let's walk over to the college library and see what we can find out about the *Lucy Belle*."

Having been to Emerson several times before, the girls were familiar with the campus. As they walked to the library building, Nancy told her companions about the riverboat book Ned had seen and the men he had overheard talking behind a stack of books.

The library was well-stocked and Mr Beecher, the head librarian, was a well-informed person.

When Nancy made her request, he replied, "Don't bother with the books we have here. There is a woman in Emerson named Mrs Palmer who can tell you more about the early history of this place than any book I've read." He jotted down her address, and the girls started for her home.

The house was on the river front a short distance from the campus. Mrs Palmer proved to be a delightful woman in her eighties. She was small in stature, with snow-white hair piled high, a delicate alabaster complexion, and a keen mind. Nancy introduced herself and her friends, explaining why Mr Beecher had sent them.

"Do come in," Mrs Palmer invited cordially. When the girls were comfortably seated in the old-fashioned parlour, the woman said, "I can tell you many stories that have been handed down." She asked how much they knew about the sinking of the *Lucy Belle*, and Nancy gave her what meagre information she had.

"That's all true," Mrs Palmer told her. "I always have felt bad to think of that gorgeous wedding gown and veil and the queen's gift of a fan being ruined by mud and water at the bottom of the river."

"Have you any idea what else was in the cargo?" Nancy asked.

"Well, rumour has it that there were two things aboard of particular value. One was the Rorick gifts. The other was a shipment of gold coins for the bank in Emerson. It's said that there was a great effort on the part of local citizens at the time to retrieve the box of coins, but if anyone ever found them, it was not reported. In any case, they never got to the bank."

The three girls were fascinated by this additional information about the *Lucy Belle*. George asked how much money was involved, but Mrs Palmer did not know.

"I'm sure it was considerable, however," she said. "There's another old rumour that a couple of crewmen had caused the explosion, stolen the gold coins, and taken off in a boat."

"Did the rumours mention any names?" Bess asked.

"I don't know. I never heard any names."

Mrs Palmer seemed to be tiring, so Nancy said that the girls had to leave now. She thanked Mrs Palmer for taking time to tell them the stories.

The elderly woman smiled. "It has been years since anyone has asked me about the early history of this place and I have been delighted to talk to you. Do come back sometime and let me relate what I have been told about the Indian raids. The old town of Emerson was plundered and burned several times, but the inhabitants loved it enough to rebuild it."

"Are many of the old families still here?" Nancy asked.

Mrs Palmer said sadly that she and Mr Rorick were the only two descendants left of the original settlers' stock. "But we helped to build the university," she said proudly, "and though that has changed the town considerably, we're glad to have done it."

Bess smiled. "We thank you for doing it. We're having a wonderful time during June Week. Will you be watching the pageant this afternoon?"

"Oh, yes," said Mrs Palmer. "A young friend is coming to take me."

After leaving, Nancy drove directly to the Rorick home. She asked her friends to help her search the books in the library for further information on the *Lucy Belle*.

"Not before lunch," Bess stated firmly. "I'm starved!"

"That seems to be a perpetual complaint of yours," said George. "What happened to that diet you were going to follow?"

Bess looked hurt. "You know I've lost seven pounds!"

"Which you'll put right back on if you don't stop stuffing yourself," George warned.

When the girls were ready to go into the library, Mrs Holman went along. As the door was swung back, the four gave startled cries. The room was a shambles! Books and pamphlets lay strewn on the floor and on the furniture.

"Mr Rorick's desk has been broken into!" exclaimed Mrs Holman.

The drawers were open. Nearly everything had been taken out of them and thrown on to the floor.

"It's the phantom!" the housekeeper said. "Why would he want to do it?"

George had a ready answer. "Maybe the phantom was so angry at finding that the money had been removed he decided to get revenge!"

There was silence for a few seconds, then Nancy said quietly, "There might be another reason for someone doing this."

The Perplexed Chief

STANDING in the midst of the untidy library, Mrs Holman, Bess, and George waited for Nancy to give her own theory as to why the phantom had made a shambles of the room.

"Don't you think," Nancy asked, "that if the only thing the mysterious thief wanted was money he would have taken all of it at once?"

"That sounds reasonable," the housekeeper conceded.

Nancy went on, "Since he simply helped himself to small amounts at a time, I believe he thought he was avoiding suspicion."

George nodded. "You mean that although Uncle John was hiding the money so that the amount was the same as the book page, he wouldn't be sure whether it was, say, a hundred and fifty or a hundred and forty that he had put in?"

"Exactly. And so he would not report the theft to the police."

Bess said, "But you haven't told us why the thief made a wreck out of this room."

Nancy replied that it was evident he was hunting for something important beside the money. "Perhaps he knows we're working on the mystery and is getting frantic to find the thing before we do."

Bess sighed. "I almost hope he found what he was looking for and never comes back!"

"That would please me too," said Mrs Holman.

As the girls picked up the books and papers they looked at each one for a clue to the mystery. The papers gave no hint, so these were put back into the desk drawers.

Bess saw something sticking from under the desk and got down on hands and knees to look. There was another paper which she pulled out and held up.

"Oh no!" she cried.

The others turned to look. On the paper were two large thumbprints.

Instantly Nancy was excited. The prints looked like the ones on the paper which had floated to her feet in the woods!

"I'll get the other paper," she said, and hurried up the stairs.

When she returned, the black prints were compared under a magnifying glass from Uncle John's desk. They were exactly the same!

"I think I should take these papers to the police," she said.

Her friends continued to hunt for clues in the books while Nancy went to town. She found Police Chief Rankin a rather stern man. Nancy stated her errand quickly and showed him the papers with the thumbprints.

After looking at them for several seconds, the officer said, "Tell me the whole story in detail."

It took Nancy some time to give him an account of what had happened since her arrival in Emerson. When she finished, Chief Rankin said, "I'm afraid I didn't put much credence in Mrs Holman's story about a phantom. As for the missing pearls, there were no fingerprints in the room but yours and hers. Frankly," he went on with an apologetic smile, "I thought it likely you had mislaid the necklace, got excited, and reported it stolen. But now I see you're not that kind of person. I will go out to Pine Hill myself and do a little investigating," he added.

"That's what I was hoping you would do," said Nancy. "When will you come?"

"Right now. I'll follow you in my car."

Mrs Holman and the girls were astonished to see Nancy drive in with the police chief. Bess whispered to the housekeeper, "Nancy's very persuasive."

After Nancy had introduced the chief to Bess and George, he gave the library a thorough inspection. The others waited patiently while he tapped the walls, looked up the chimney, and asked if there were a trap door under any of the rugs.

Bess whispered to George, "Nancy has already done all this. Why don't we tell him so?"

"Better not," her cousin replied. She smiled. "We might be interfering with his—er—duties!"

When the officer finished, he said firmly, "There's only one possible way a thief could have entered this room. He must have a duplicate key to the padlock."

"But, Chief Rankin," Mrs Holman spoke up, "there is only one key to this padlock and the man at the lock shop assured Mr Rorick that the padlock could not be picked."

Chief Rankin frowned. He did not argue with the housekeeper, but said crisply, "Take my advice—put a new padlock on at once and don't let anyone get hold of the key to it!"

Mrs Holman was a bit hurt by his peremptory manner, but she merely said, "I will do that." Turning to Nancy, she asked, "Would you have time to run downtown and buy a new padlock?"

Nancy glanced at her wrist watch. It was just one o'clock and the girls were not due at the pageant until four. "I'll have plenty of time," she told the housekeeper.

As she went outdoors with Chief Rankin, he said that he would look round the grounds, although he did not think he would find anything helpful.

"Footprints wouldn't mean anything. There must be hundreds of them around here, with people cutting grass, gardening, and searching for clues." As he spoke the latter phrase, he looked significantly at Nancy.

She smiled in answer, then asked, "What about the bobbing light in the woods at night?"

"Have you seen it yourself?" the officer asked.

"Yes."

Chief Rankin rubbed his chin thoughtfully. "I feel sure that no thief is going to give away his position by walking round those woods with a flashlight. I'd say they're used by people who are taking shortcuts from the beach to the road."

Nancy did not comment—the police chief might be right! She said goodbye, thanked him for coming, and drove off to get the new padlock. She obtained one at Emerson's largest ironmongery. The owner assured her that the lock was the very latest model and positively could not be opened except with the proper key.

"Not even by a locksmith?" Nancy asked, her eyes twinkling.

"Well," said the shop owner, "I wouldn't go so far as to say that. But it would take a real expert to figure this one out. What are you going to use it for?"

Nancy was vague in her answer. "Put it on a certain door to keep out burglars," she said, chuckling, and the man did not ask any more questions.

She paid for the padlock and hurried home. Mrs Holman predicted that even two locks on the library door were not going to keep out the phantom. Nevertheless, she permitted Nancy and George to install the new lock to which there were two keys. She took one herself, and suggested that Nancy take the other and hide it carefully.

During her absence, Bess and George had been looking through volume after volume of Uncle John's books. But most of them had nothing to do with old boats or the history of the area.

Soon Mrs Holman announced that luncheon was ready and the girls went into the dining-room. There were cold cuts, potato salad, large, ripe tomatoes, and a delicious chocolate mousse dessert.

"You are a marvellous cook," Nancy said to Mrs Holman. "Everything is so good!"

The girls insisted upon washing the dishes. While they were working, there was a knock on the back door and

Bess opened it. Fred Jenkins walked in, grinning at the three girls.

"Hi, everybody!" he said. "I've got to work fast around here today, because I want to see that pageant, too."

Mrs Holman appeared and told him to vacuum the living-room, then the hall.

"Okay," he said, and went off to do it.

As soon as the girls had finished their dishwashing chore, they went back to the library to look at more books. Mrs Holman accompanied them, a mop and dustcloth in her hands.

Fred, coming into the hall, saw her. "Oh, you shouldn't be doing that," he said. "I'll clean the library for you."

"No, thank you," said the housekeeper. "Mr Rorick doesn't want anybody but me to work in the room."

At that moment Fred noticed the two padlocks on the door. He began to laugh. "You sure must have a gold mine in that place." The others ignored him.

As he worked in the hall, Mrs Holman kept an eye on him. Each time he came near the door to the library, she went out and found him another job which took him away from it.

"He's too nosey," she said to the girls.

Presently the telephone rang and Mrs Holman answered it. After a short conversation, she hung up and came to the library door. The housekeeper beckoned Nancy towards her and whispered:

"That was Chief Rankin. He said to tell you that the thumbprints on that paper are not on record. Whoever left them is not a known criminal."

"That makes our job even harder," Nancy commented.

By this time Fred had finished all the work which the housekeeper wanted him to do indoors that day. She told him to go outside and weed the garden.

Nancy and the housekeeper returned to the library. By this time the girls had gone through hundreds of books.

Suddenly Bess called out excitedly, "A clue! I've found a clue!"

· 8 ·

Indian Attack

Bess had been seated on top of a small ladder reading one of the very old books she had found. Now she jumped down and showed it to the others.

"There's a whole article about the *Lucy Belle*," she said. "And pasted in the back of the book is this."

She pointed to a list of names, all men. Scrawled across the bottom of the sheet was the notation, "Survivors of the *Lucy Belle*."

"Oh, Bess," Nancy cried out, "this is a wonderful find!" She began to count the names—there were nine. "Does it say in the article where the men went?"

"No, it doesn't," Bess replied. "It tells about the construction of the *Lucy Belle*, which was a combination freight and passenger steamboat."

"Then it doesn't mention the cargo?"

"No."

"Girls," said Nancy, "if we hurry, we'll have time to stop at Mrs Palmer's before we go to the pageant. Let's see if she can identify any of these names."

Bess wanted to know what good that would do. "Those men have been dead a long time."

"But they may have left families," Nancy replied. "Maybe one or more of their descendants are around

61

here and trying to find a clue to that treasure of coins."

"You mean," said Bess, "that one of them is the phantom?"

"Possibly."

After Nancy copied the names, the three girls dressed quickly and set off for Mrs Palmer's home. She was surprised to see them so soon again, but appeared delighted. "I can tell by your eyes, Nancy, that you have more questions for me."

Nancy smiled and produced the list of *Lucy Belle* survivors.

The elderly woman eyed it in amazement. "You are real sleuths," she complimented her visitors.

Mrs Palmer settled down in an armchair to study the list. Finally she went to a bookcase, and pulled out a thin volume which she said was the genealogy of the old families of Emerson. She went through each page carefully, comparing the names on it with those which Nancy had brought.

Presently she said, "I believe I have found something!"

"Yes?" Nancy asked, leaning forward eagerly.

The elderly woman said that two names in the book were identical with two on the list, although they were several generations apart. "It's just possible that the younger ones are descendants of these survivors."

"Do they live in Emerson now?" Nancy asked.

"Well, yes and no. There are two young men at the university whose families used to reside here but moved away. Their names are Tom Akin and Ben Farmer."

The three girls exclaimed in surprise. "Why, Tom and Ben are Omegas!" George said.

Mrs Palmer smiled. "You're familiar with that fraternity?"

Nancy told her about Ned, Dave, and Burt inviting them for June Week. "Maybe the boys can give us some good leads," she added.

Unable to restrain her enthusiasm, Nancy asked if she might use Mrs Palmer's telephone. "Help yourself, my dear."

On the chance that Tom and Ben might still be at the Omega House, Nancy called it. To her delight, both of them were there. Quickly she explained why she had called.

Tom, who had answered the phone, said that indeed he was a direct descendant of the Tom Akin who was a survivor of the *Lucy Belle*. "I believe he was one of the officers."

Nancy asked that when the boys had a chance they tell her all they knew about the history of the sunken ship. "We'll be more than glad to. Say, you girls have no dates for the afternoon, have you? . . . Well, we're in the same boat. Our friends are in the pageant, too. How about sitting with us? Then Ben and I will tell you all we know."

"Marvellous!" said Nancy. "We'll be in the first row —Ned suggested that. Will you meet us there?"

"We'll go right now and save seats," Tom offered.

Before leaving Mrs Palmer, Nancy planted a kiss of thanks on the woman's cheek. "You've been a wonderful help. If I ever solve the mystery, I'll come back to tell you."

Mrs Palmer smiled. "I hope that's a promise."

When the girls arrived at the waterfront, Tom and

Ben were already there. As promised, the boys had saved three seats in the front row.

Almost at once, Tom gave an account of the sinking of the *Lucy Belle*. Both he and Ben had heard stories about it, but these did not differ from what the girls knew.

"I've heard, however," Ben said, "that my forebear survived the shipwreck, only to be massacred later with some of the other survivors near the Indian village. He had left his wife and son in Pittsburgh, but afterwards they came here to visit relatives and remained."

"Killed by Indians! How awful!" exclaimed Bess.

"The white men must have provoked them," Ben said. "Except for this one incident, they were friendly with the settlers at that time."

George remarked, "What seems strange to me is that nobody has tried to retrieve the sunken treasure."

"You mean the gold coins?" Tom asked. When George nodded, he said, "Oh, some of the college boys have tried in the past few years since scuba diving has become popular. Ben and I have been down several times."

"You didn't find any trace of them?" Nancy queried.

Tom laughed. "We couldn't even find the ship. Maybe we didn't have the right location, but everyone around here thinks the *Lucy Belle* is sunk so deep in the mud that she'll never be found. You know, the bottom of this tributary is really an underwater valley between the two shores."

There was silence for a few moments, then suddenly Nancy asked, "Is it possible to hire diving equipment in Emerson?"

Tom and Ben seemed startled by the question, but Tom answered. "Yes, it is. Don't tell me you're going to try to find the *Lucy Belle*!"

Nancy laughed. "I just might do that."

For the next few minutes Nancy and her friends studied the printed programme. There was to be a succession of floats showing how Emerson had developed from a wilderness into a university town. First came flatboats on which the earliest merchants sent their goods up into the wilderness territory.

Next came the keelboats, called barges, which ran on regular schedules as the population increased.

Presently George called out, "Here comes Burt!"

She began to giggle as she saw him playing the part of a fully bearded captain in an old-fashioned uniform and cap. He was standing on a barge with one arm outstretched in front of him, directing his crew where to take their load of iron ore.

The programme said that there had been a forge in the area where smelting was done. These forges formed little communities where the smith, his family, and his workers lived.

Suddenly Bess burst into laughter. "Oh, I can't believe it! Look at Dave!"

Her friend, wearing a bushy-haired wig, whiskers, and sideburns, was in charge of an ark filled with animals! Squealing pigs, mooing cows, and neighing horses apparently were very unhappy and Dave was having a hectic time with several helpers trying to keep the creatures quiet.

"No wonder he wouldn't tell me what part he was going to play," said Bess. "He'll never live this down!"

There were many other types of early river transportation in the parade, including one showing a shipment of salt. Other floats depicted a church and an early school building.

The last number was an elaborate one. In a disreputable shantyboat stood a crude shack. Through a large window, in a scene lighted by old-fashioned lanterns, a miser could be seen. He was seated at a table counting a large heap of coins.

Trailing the shantyboat was a large pirogue. The dugout was filled with Indians, and Ned was playing the part of their chief. As the boats neared the seated spectators, Ned and his party sneaked aboard the shantyboat, robbed the miser of his coins, and tossed the man into the water!

Quickly the Indians climbed back into their pirogue and headed for shore. It landed directly in front of Nancy's group.

Ned leaped out, and giving a war whoop rushed up to Nancy, scooped her up in his arms, and raced back to his dugout with her.

"Ned, stop it!" Nancy cried in embarrassment. "Stop it!"

She tried to struggle free, but Ned's Indian companions helped hold her and paddled off quickly. The crowd of onlookers, sure that this was part of the programme, cheered loudly.

"Ned, where are you going? What are you doing?" Nancy cried out.

Ned rose to his full height and said in a stentorian voice, "Big Chief take pretty maiden to treasure spot!"

· 9 ·

Ancient Stump

THE pirogue was quickly paddled across the cove. Nancy asked where they were going.

Ned, with a grin, said in his natural voice. "Around the corner of Pine Hill. After you girls had left the house, Mrs Holman telephoned me. The fellows found me in the gym, where I was being made up. She said Uncle John Rorick had called and wanted to talk to you, Nancy."

"Did he give her the message?" Nancy asked.

"Yes. He wants you girls to stay longer than Sunday afternoon—in fact, he wants you to stay until you solve the mystery."

Nancy laughed. "He's taking a great chance. Who knows how long we may be in Emerson?"

"That's great with me," said Ned. "Starting from Monday we'll be studying hard because exams are the week after next, but a few dates would ease the strain on the brain!"

Nancy said she was sure Bess and George had nothing special to take them home and they would stay a few days longer, at least. Then she added, "But what does this have to do with the treasure you're going to show me?"

Ned explained that while Uncle John was talking to Mr Holman, he had suddenly remembered having heard his parents mention an old pine tree in connection with the *Lucy Belle*. He had been a young child at the time and did not understand what had been meant by the remark. Now he wondered if a pine tree might prove to be a clue.

"Ned, you mean to say you've found that pine?" Nancy said excitedly "Oh, where? How?"

Ned answered that he recalled having seen a large pine stump embedded in the embankment just round the bend of Pine Hill. "I thought that might be the one, so my friends and I brought some digging tools to find the lost treasure."

The paddlers put on speed and in a few minutes came to the spot. Everyone stepped from the pirogue and the boys began their work.

After fifteen minutes had gone by and nothing had been unearthed, one of the boys said, "I guess those old war-whoopers—or the crewmen—made away with everything worth while."

The others laughed, but Ned urged him not to give up yet. "Don't you want a share of the wampum?" he asked.

The boys widened their location of operations. They were silent for some time, during which Nancy ambled around, trying to reconstruct the scene of the sinking *Lucy Belle* and the survivors getting to shore. Was this a likely place for them to have landed, she wondered.

Suddenly one of the boys yelled and Nancy turned to see why. "Look!" he exclaimed, and held up an anchor.

The others rushed forward to examine it. The anchor was covered with rust, which the boys began to chip off with their tools.

Secretly Nancy felt that the anchor was too small to have been used on the *Lucy Belle*. Nevertheless, she watched eagerly and finally an indistinct name came to light. It was *Rover*.

The finder rubbed his perspiring brow. "All this work for nothing!"

Ned conceded defeat. He told Nancy he was sorry to have misled her, but that he had been sure he had discovered a good clue.

Nancy smiled at him. "Don't feel bad," she said. "I enjoyed being kidnapped by Indians and it has given me an idea."

"I hope it's a better one than mine," Ned said disconsolately.

He and his friends were a sorry-looking sight. They were hot, dirty, and tired. Dust and mud had spattered on their grease-painted bodies and those who had not removed their wigs were now wearing them askew. Nancy found it hard to keep from laughing.

"Let's go back to the gym," said one of them.

"Okay," Ned agreed. "Hop in, Nancy."

She shook her head. "If you don't mind, since I'm so close to the house, I think I'll walk through the woods." She took her car keys from her bag and handed them to Ned. "Would you mind giving these to Bess and George and telling them where I am?"

Ned looked at her for several seconds, then said, "You'll be safer if I go with you. That phantom may be spying on you again." He handed the keys to one of the other boys. "See that Bess and George get these, will you?"

The pirogue pushed off and the couple climbed the embankment. As they started through the pine grove, Ned said, "What is this great idea you mentioned?"

Nancy replied that she had been thinking over the historical facts she had gleaned from the pageant and concluded there were many Indians not far from Pine Hill during those days.

"That probably means they came from their village to the water. Some of their braves may have found loot washed ashore from the ship and carried it away with them."

"Maybe," said Ned. "Can't you see some Indian maiden wearing Miss Abigail Rorick's wedding dress?"

Nancy laughed. "Just the same, I'm going to try to find an antique map of this area and see if an Indian village is marked on it."

"Where are you going to look?" Ned queried.

"In Uncle John's library."

Ned said, "Suppose you tell me what you think might have happened after the sinking of the *Lucy Belle*."

"Well," Nancy began, "if the Indians stole valuable cargo, they might have buried it so that they could pretend innocence."

"That sounds logical," Ned said. "Go on."

"It's also possible that the survivors of the *Lucy Belle*, fearing they might be attacked by marauders, hid their reserve cargo underground near the Indian village. That would be an easy spot to find again."

"Well, I certainly wish you luck," Ned said. He grinned wearily. "I'm glad you're not going to ask me to do any more digging tonight. But when you find that map let me know."

He took the lead on the way to the house, but suddenly he and Nancy stood stock-still. From somewhere in the grove came an ear-piercing shriek of terror.

"Where did that come from?" Ned asked worriedly.

"Someone may have been attacked!" Nancy exclaimed.

She lay on the ground to listen for footsteps. Nancy heard them receding in the direction from which she and Ned had come. The couple ran that way but saw no one. Finally Nancy stopped and put her ear to the ground again. She could no longer hear footfalls. Swiftly she and Ned searched the grove but found no sign of a victim.

"More likely he got a glimpse of you and was terrified that he had seen an Indian warrior," Nancy teased.

"It wouldn't surprise me," Ned said, "if your phantom made that outcry just to scare us away."

"I wonder where he went," Nancy mused.

Once more the couple turned towards the house. When they reached it a few minutes later, they discovered that Mrs Holman had not yet returned from the pageant and the house was tightly locked.

"She should be along soon," said Nancy. "Let's sit down and wait."

Wearily she and Ned flopped on to the steps of the rear porch. It was not long before the housekeeper drove up in a friend's car. She smiled upon seeing Ned and suggested that he take off his disguise before going back to town.

He laughed. "If I keep this up, poor Uncle John won't have any clothes left!"

He went upstairs, took a shower, and a little while later appeared in clothes which Uncle John evidently wore when he was working in the garden.

While he had been changing, Nancy had suggested to Mrs Holman that they open both padlocks on the library door and look in. As they entered, Nancy exclaimed in horror:

"Oh no!"

All the books had been taken from the shelves and thrown helter-skelter around the room!

Mrs Holman wrung her hands. "It's the phantom again!" she exclaimed. "Every door and window in this house was tightly locked before I left!"

Ned joined them. "Wow-ee!" he exclaimed, then frowned. "Whoever did this must be desperate to find what he's looking for."

"The question is, was he successful?" Mrs Holman asked.

Nancy did not reply. She had noticed a rolled parchment on the floor beside Mr Rorick's desk. Quickly she went over, picked up the parchment, and opened it carefully. Engraved on it was a very old map showing the Emerson area in the eighteenth century. Nancy's face lighted up.

"Here's what I was going to search for!" she said excitedly.

· 10 ·

The Camouflaged Door

A CAR door slammed outside the Rorick house. Nancy, Ned, and Mrs Holman looked out to see who had arrived.

"It's Bess and George," the housekeeper said. "Why don't you wait until they come in and tell all of us what you've discovered, Nancy?"

"I will," she answered, as Mrs Holman went to open the front door.

"Is Nancy here? Is she all right?" Bess asked quickly.

The woman assured her that Nancy was fine and had enjoyed being kidnapped by the Indians. The three entered the book-strewn library.

"Gosh!" exclaimed George. "Another visit from the phantom?"

Quickly Nancy explained, then told the girls of Uncle John's request that they stay to work on the mystery.

"Okay with me," said George. Bess nodded, but she did not look happy.

"Now tell us what happened to you, Nancy," George urged.

Ned stepped forward and laid a hand on Nancy's

shoulder. "Meet Indian Princess Nonaviki," he said solemnly. "She help Chief solve heap-big Indian mystery."

Everyone laughed, but Bess said, "Oh, do be serious. What's the discovery, Nancy?"

The young sleuth pointed to the parchment. "According to this, there was once an Indian village about a mile from here. I had a hunch today that there might be one connected with our mystery."

Ned interrupted to say, "Nancy got this idea after a boo-boo I pulled." He told about the fiasco of the stump.

"Why, I think the pine tree was a very good clue," Bess said kindly. "But now you believe the gold coins may be buried in or near the old Indian village?"

"Yes, I do," Nancy replied. "The thieves probably would have buried them as soon as possible. And then, too, those crewmen might have offered some coins to friendly Indians in return for a good hiding place. The village would be a logical location."

"Tell you what," said Ned. "Suppose we go out to that old Indian village after chapel."

"That's a wonderful idea," Nancy said enthusiastically.

Ned said he would have to be excused to go back to the fraternity house. "May I borrow your car, Nancy? I'll be back for you at seven o'clock with Burt and Dave." She nodded.

Mrs Holman, Bess, and George had already started to pick up books and return them to the shelves.

After Ned had left, Nancy sat down to study the old map. She was so deeply engrossed in it that Bess and

George had to urge her three times to put it away and dress for the Omega dinner dance.

"I overheard some of the boys talking and I think there's going to be a big surprise tonight," Bess said mysteriously.

"Have you any idea what it is?" George asked.

"Not the slightest. But it's a secret they're going to spring on the guests."

When they reached their rooms, Bess and George began to conjecture what the surprise might be. Nancy, lost in thought about the Indian village and the chance that at last she might have hit upon an excellent clue, did not join in the conversation, though the connecting door was open.

Again, she was the first one dressed. This time she had chosen a turquoise gown with a slightly full skirt. It was quite plain except for an intriguing geometric design in brilliant colours embroidered on one side of the bodice. The trimming reached from the shoulders to the waistline.

Bess and George looked equally attractive—Bess in pink, George wearing a flowing black chiffon gown.

By the time the girls grabbed their wraps and came downstairs their dates had arrived. All of them whistled in admiration upon seeing the girls.

"You look super!" cried Dave. He glanced at Nancy. "Some Indian princess!"

Nancy laughed and patted Ned's arm. "The Indian Chief looks a bit dressed up too, don't you think?"

When they reached the Omega House, the teasing continued. The main topic of conversation before dinner was the kidnapping of the Indian princess. The fun did not stop until chimes sounded, announcing dinner.

The members and their guests went to the dining-room and found their chairs by place cards. Nancy and Ned were seated directly in front of the speakers' table.

The president of the fraternity, Chuck Wilson, sat down and everyone began to eat. It was nearly an hour later when he arose and signalled for attention.

"We're going to have a little business meeting now," he said with a grin. "A special one." He called on the fraternity secretary.

A serious-faced, bespectacled youth stood up and announced that two alumni members had left sizeable sums of money to the fraternity chapter.

"Now we can start building our new house," he said gleefully. Loud applause followed this exciting announcement.

"Was this the big secret?" Nancy whispered to Ned.

"I don't know. To tell the truth, I didn't hear until this afternoon that some important news would be released this evening."

When the room was quiet again, the president rose once more and said he would call on the nominating chairman to announce the officers for the following year. The Committee had felt it would be interesting for the boys' dates as well as the members to hear the results.

A husky boy, seated next to him, stood up and smiled at his audience. "I'm going to reverse the usual order," he said, "and tell you last who our new president will be." He read the name of the treasurer who would take office, then the corresponding secretary, the recording secretary, and the vice-president.

He now paused and looked over the whole room. An eager member finally called out, "Well, who is it?"

"For your next president there was only one dissenting vote. That came from himself! Modest guy! So really by unanimous vote the next president of Omega Chi Epsilon Fraternity of Emerson University is—Ned Nickerson!"

"Oh, Ned," cried Nancy, "that's simply wonderful!" She grasped his hand and kissed him.

Ned looked stunned. For a moment he seemed overwhelmed. Then as cries of "Speech! Speech!" and terrific clapping rang in his ears, he got to his feet and faced his fellow members.

"You certainly caught me off balance this time," he said. Gradually his usual composure returned and he said seriously, "Thanks, fellows. It's going to be mighty hard filling Chuck Wilson's shoes. You all know that. I'll try hard, however." He smiled. "Just don't make it too rough for me, all of you!" He sat down.

There was more applause, then the outgoing president took charge. "Ned, I'll turn the gavel over to you after the private induction ceremonies next week. In the meantime, my personal congratulations and good luck, brother."

Nancy was wondering about the private induction. This was one thing she would never learn about, she knew, but it would be a memory Ned would cherish all his life. She herself was bursting with pride as everyone in the room rushed up to shake Ned's hand and wish him well. By the time they finished, he was blushing over the compliments.

At nine o'clock a small band arrived and started

off with a lively dance number. Soon the floor, from which the tables had been cleared, was filled with swaying, happy couples.

The wonderful evening ended very late. But early the next morning Nancy was awakened by a knock on her door.

"Come in!" she called sleepily.

Mrs Holman entered and apologized for waking her guest. She extended an envelope to Nancy, saying, "I thought this might be important. I found it on the hall floor. It must have been pushed under the front door."

Nancy glanced at the crude printing of her name. Her first thought was that it might be a joke. Quickly she pulled out the sheet of paper from the envelope. When she read the note, also crudely printed, she was inclined to believe the writer meant the warning it contained. The note said:

GO HOME AT ONCE.
DANGER FROM THE PHANTOM.

Bess and George had also heard the knock on Nancy's door and now came into her room. When they read the note, Bess became worried.

"You've been all right so far, Nancy. Don't stretch your luck. I think we'd better go home after the picnic today."

Nancy shook her head. "And disappoint Mr Rorick? It's my guess that whoever wrote this note overheard some conversation about Uncle John's invitation to us to stay longer and find the phantom. The eavesdropper was hoping we would leave today."

George voted to stay. "I'd like to catch this spy. He

probably listens on the extension phones and—"

"And can go through walls!" Bess added significantly.

The girls' remarks gave Nancy a new idea. "There
may be hideaways in the parts of this house we haven't
searched. Mrs Holman, will you take me all over so I
can hunt for them?"

"I'll be glad to, but how about you girls having some
breakfast?"

This was agreed upon and the trio dressed quickly in
order to do some searching before going to chapel.
Nancy slipped into a pair of blue slacks and a matching
polo-neck sweater, then hurried downstairs.

Since Bess and George were not ready, Nancy and
Mrs Holman went to search the attic. Neither of them
found any hidden rooms, secret doors, or sliding panels.
Next, they looked through the first floor without
success.

"The only place left is the cellar," Nancy said. "I'll
dash down there myself while you get breakfast." The
housekeeper nodded.

Nancy snapped on the cellar light and descended the
old-fashioned stairway. The place was cool and slightly
musty. Nancy found many storage nooks and cubby-
holes, but none revealed a hideaway.

At the far end of the cellar Nancy saw an intriguing
workshop. She pulled the chain of the old-fashioned
ceiling light. The room was filled with old tools, but a
heavy layer of dust and many cobwebs indicated that
the place had not been used for some time.

"That proves the phantom is not interested in it," she
said to herself.

Nancy began to tap the walls behind the various workbenches. There was nothing suspicious about them, but she did notice one section of another wooden wall which had nothing in front of it. Curious, she tapped it.

"This sounds hollow!" she decided excitedly.

Her deft fingers went all over the woodwork and suddenly she found a cleverly concealed latch. She tried to lift the latch, but it would not budge. To jar it loose, Nancy struck the wood next to it. A second later the door to the workshop slammed shut. Intent on what she thought she was about to discover, the young detective paid no attention to this, but tried the hidden latch again. She heard it click and gave the secret door a hard —and disastrous—yank.

The next instant the whole section of wall came towards her. It hit Nancy hard, knocking her down. She blacked out!

· 11 ·

Treasure Hunters

BREAKFAST was ready, so Mrs Holman called down to Nancy from the top of the cellar stairs. There was no answer. She called more loudly, but still there was no response. "Whatever is Nancy doing?" the housekeeper wondered.

At that moment Bess and George came into the kitchen. She asked them to try their luck getting the young sleuth to come up and eat.

"Nancy! N-A-N-C-Y!"

When they received no reply, the two girls went downstairs to find their friend. To their surprise, she was not in sight. They kept calling and investigating each storage nook. Finally they came to the closed door of the workshop.

"Nancy must be in there," said George, and gave the door a yank. It would not open.

George called loudly through the crack. Nancy did not answer, and suddenly Bess went ash white. "Oh, I'm sure something has happened to her!"

"She must be in the room behind this door," George said grimly. "The question is, did she lock it or did someone else?"

Tears began to roll down Bess's cheeks. "The phantom carried out his threat! She's a prisoner!"

George set her jaw grimly. "We must get inside!"

There was no lock on the door, so the girls assumed it must be fastened on the inside. They tried ramming their bodies against it, but the heavy wooden door would not budge.

By this time Mrs Holman had descended the steps. Upon hearing what Bess and George suspected, she instantly became alarmed.

"How can we get in here?" Bess asked.

"I don't know. That's an old workshop and there's a heavy wooden bar that locks it on the inside."

Bess said, "I'm sure Nancy didn't lock herself in. Oh, maybe she is l-lying in there injured!"

"Maybe not," said the housekeeper, trying to be calm. "Sometimes when that door swings shut, the big bar inside falls into place. If Nancy was hammering on the walls, the vibration could have made the door close. But Nancy should be able to raise the bar."

"And why doesn't she answer us?" Bess wailed.

George said, "Mrs Holman, do you have a big hammer handy?"

"There's one in the kitchen. I'll get it."

She vanished up the stairway but returned in half a minute with the hammer. George swung it heftily, trying to knock off the heavy old-time hinges. They were so deeply embedded in the wood that she could make no impression.

Bess spoke up, her voice trembling, "Mrs Holman, is there a window from the outside that opens into that workshop?"

The housekeeper shook her head. "There's no entrance to that room except from here."

"Have you a thin saw that we could put through this crack?" George asked.

"I think so. I'll look."

Five minutes elapsed before Mrs Holman came downstairs and handed a dull, rusty saw to George. The girl wedged it through the crack. She could feel the obstructing wooden bar, but though she tried hard, George could not saw through it.

Bess complained, "Oh, why can't we do something?"

"Crying won't help any," George said severely to her cousin. "Put on your thinking cap!"

Chastened, Bess thought quickly and said, "Why don't we get a hatchet or an axe and hack down the door?"

"Now you're using your head," said George. "Mrs Holman, can you produce one of those tools?"

The housekeeper was not sure but said she would look in the garage. Fortunately she found a sharp axe. George grabbed it in both hands, gave a mighty heave, and landed it on the door. There was a distinct sound of cracking wood.

Twice more she aimed at the same spot. On the third try the axe crashed all the way through. There was an opening large enough for her to put her hand through and raise the bar.

Bess pulled the door open, then gave a shriek. Across the room Nancy lay on the floor unconscious, a heavy door partly covering her body. Beyond was a gaping hole to the garden!

Mrs Holman and the two girls rushed over to Nancy.

As Bess and George lifted the door away, Mrs Holman knelt down and felt the girl's pulse. At that moment Nancy stirred.

"She's coming round!" the housekeeper said.

"Thank goodness!" Bess murmured. She crouched and ran her fingers through Nancy's hair. "Oh, Nancy, Nancy, whatever happened to you?"

Her friend did not reply. It was several minutes before she opened her eyes and looked round. She seemed to be in a daze.

"I'll get some water," Mrs Holman offered.

The soothing, cool water soon revived Nancy and in halting tones she told what had happened to her.

"Do you think the phantom did it?" Bess asked Nancy.

"No. There was no one in this room."

Mrs Holman said she thought Nancy should go upstairs and lie down. "I'm going to ask the university doctor to come in and examine you," she stated.

Nancy was sure she would be all right. "I'm just a bit bruised." But the housekeeper insisted.

She put an arm around Nancy to help her upstairs. At the housekeeper's suggestion, Bess and George stayed behind to set the hidden door in place. For the first time they noticed how unusual the outside of it was. Very thin pieces of stone had been wedged into the wood. When the door was in place, it would look as if it were part of the foundation. The two girls searched, but they found nothing to indicate that the door could be opened from the outside.

"I'll bet it was for escape in case of Indian attack," George remarked, as the girls walked to the kitchen stairway. The cousins found Nancy in the living-room, resting on the couch. After they told her about the camouflaged door, she said, "Anyway, the phantom didn't use it. That door hadn't been opened in years!"

Within fifteen minutes Dr Smith arrived and with him, Ned Nickerson, whom he had called, knowing that Ned was a special friend.

Ned rushed up to Nancy, a look of deep concern on his face. "Thank goodness you weren't killed!" he exclaimed.

Dr Smith came to the girl's side. "Oh tush! Miss Drew looks far from killed!"

He insisted that Nancy go upstairs, where he would make a thorough examination. The others waited tensely. Although Nancy had seemed all right, they knew how brave she was and that she might be hiding some really serious trouble so as not to worry her friends.

Mrs Holman asked if any of them would like to eat, but they shook their heads. Bess managed a wry smile. "For once in my life I've lost my appetite."

When Dr Smith came downstairs, Ned and the girls jumped up eagerly. "How is she?" they asked in unison.

The physician smiled. "I'm glad to give you a good report. No broken bones. A few bruises, but so far as I can determine, she suffered no serious injuries. I want Miss Drew to stay in bed at least until tomorrow morning. She didn't like it much when I told her this, because it seems she had great plans for the day."

"I'm sure they can wait," said Mrs Holman.

"May we see her and can she eat breakfast?" Bess asked quickly.

"I suggest that you give her one hour by herself. It's a shock to the system when one gets knocked out. Miss Drew will make a quick comeback, I'm sure, but sleep will help her. As for eating, only a light diet to-day."

Keeping as quiet as possible, they sat down and ate their own breakfast. Bess and George briefed Ned on what the young detective had been doing when the accident happened.

"Another false clue," George said with a sigh.

"We must get that secret door nailed shut," said Mrs Holman, "so that the phantom can't use it." Ned volunteered to do the job. After finishing it, he left.

At the end of the doctor's prescribed hour, the girls went to Nancy's room. She was awake and demanded something to eat.

"Coming right up!" said George, delighted that colour had returned to her friend's face and once more her eyes were sparkling.

She went downstairs to get orange juice, a soft-boiled egg, and some toast. When she returned, Nancy suggested that Bess and George go to chapel. "You don't have to stay with me. I'm perfectly all right. Take my car."

Bess and George followed her suggestion. They quickly freshened up, took off their slacks, and put on dresses. A few minutes later they were on their way to chapel.

Presently Mrs Holman came upstairs and Nancy said to her, "Early tomorrow morning I'm going to that Indian village shown on the map. I just can't wait to do a little investigating there." She was sorry that the boys would have to study the next day and could not accompany them.

The following morning Nancy felt fully recovered. As soon as she and her friends could get away after breakfast, they started for the Indian village, taking digging tools with them. They walked to the cove, then followed the direction indicated on the old map. Finally they came to a clearing which Nancy figured had once been the site of a thriving community. Here and there on the landscape were large weed-covered humps.

"What were they for?" Bess asked.

"It's my guess," Nancy said, "that those were the clay ovens where the Indians baked their bread. Now the weeds have taken over."

After hunting around for a while, the girls picked up a few arrowheads, but apart from this evidence there was nothing to indicate that there had ever been a tribal settlement at this spot.

"We came to find a treasure and maybe a lost wedding dress," Bess reminded the others. "I'm sure we're never going to in this place."

The other girls were not so sure. George said, "If you were an Indian, where would you hide a treasure?"

Nancy thought for a few moments, then answered, "In a sacred place where other Indians would be too superstitious to touch it."

"That sounds reasonable," Bess agreed. "I've read that the sacred building or ground in an Indian village was sometimes right in the centre."

"That's true," said Nancy. She walked around and finally picked a spot which might once have been the centre of the village. "Let's start digging here."

As they picked up their tools, the girls became aware of a young man walking towards them. He was Fred Jenkins.

"So you're digging for Indian relics, eh?" he asked. "I have a message for you, Miss Nancy," he said.

"For me? From whom?" she asked.

"Your father. He called up and I wrote it out. I thought I'd better get it to you right away." He handed a small sheet of paper to Nancy.

Written on it was a badly spelled message. Nancy caught her breath as she read:

"I need you at home at once. Hannah Gruen is very ill."

· 12 ·

A Frightening Message

"When did this message come?" Nancy asked Fred Jenkins.

He thought a moment, then answered, " 'Bout half an hour or so ago. I was cleaning the ground floor and answered the phone—Mrs Holman was busy upstairs and didn't hear it. Your father said he wanted you to get the message right away, so I asked her where you were. She told me where this place was and I figured I'd come and tell you!"

"That was very kind of you," said Nancy. "Girls, it's too bad to leave here, but you know how I feel about Hannah. We'll have to go right home."

Fred was staring at Nancy intently. "I'm terribly sorry I brought you bad news. I hope the lady will get well soon."

As the girls gathered up their tools, Fred added, "I'll miss seeing you all around. Kind of got used to you."

As Nancy and her friends started towards the cove Fred walked ahead of them. In a few minutes he had vanished among the trees.

"I wonder what happened to Mrs Gruen," said Bess. "She seemed to be in the best of health when we left home."

"Perhaps it was an accident," George ventured.

Nancy's expression was grim and she did not comment until they had reached the garden behind the house.

"As soon as we get inside, I'm going to phone River Heights. If something did happen to Hannah, I want to know what it is."

Bess looked at Nancy, puzzled. "*If*—?"

Nancy nodded. "This whole thing could be a hoax."

"But why?" Bess queried.

"To get rid of us. The phantom could have made that phone call so we'd leave Pine Hill."

"In other words," George spoke up, "you're learning a little too much here to please this mysterious thief."

"Possibly," Nancy answered. "But there could be another reason for a fake phone call."

"What's that?" Bess asked.

Nancy said that if the phantom was hunting for the same thing the girls were—the gold coins and the Rorick wedding gifts—then he might have wanted to find out where the girls were sleuthing at the moment. Knowing the set-up of the Drew family, he had invented the story as an excuse for Fred to get information from Mrs Holman.

"And the caller may have followed Fred?" George asked.

"Yes."

By this time the girls had reached the back door. Mrs Holman admitted them. At once she expressed her sympathy over what had happened and said she hoped Mrs Gruen's illness was not serious.

"I'm going to find out at once," said Nancy, and went to the hall telephone.

She dialled the number of her home, tapping her foot impatiently as she waited for someone to answer. After several rings Hannah Gruen's voice came over the wire, clear and strong.

"Hannah!" cried Nancy. "Are you all right?"

The Drews' housekeeper chuckled. "I never felt better in my life. Why the concern, Nancy?"

The young sleuth stammered as she told the whole story.

"Well, there's not one word of truth in it," Mrs Gruen declared. "And I can't see why anyone would have made up such a wild tale."

When Nancy told her the theories she had, Mrs Gruen sighed. "I only hope you're in no danger, dear," she said worriedly. "Perhaps you ought to take the hint and come home."

"Oh, I can't do that!" Nancy replied. "No phantom is going to give me orders!"

Mrs Gruen laughed heartily. "If the whole matter weren't serious, Nancy," she said, "that would be an utterly ridiculous statement."

Suddenly Nancy realized how strange her remark must have sounded. She, too, laughed but said, "And if he's hiding somewhere near and can hear what I'm saying, I hope he knows I mean every word of it!"

Nancy learned from Hannah Gruen that Mr Drew was out of town, but that he had phoned home to learn where Nancy was and what she was doing.

"When will you be home?" Hannah asked.

"Not for a few more days," Nancy told her. "Mr Rorick wants us to stay until we solve the mystery."

Mrs Gruen said she hoped it would not take much

longer. "It's mighty lonesome around here without you."

"I miss you, too," Nancy told her. Then she described Mrs Holman and ended by saying, "She makes us feel quite at home."

After Nancy had hung up, Mrs Holman complained that Fred had not yet returned. "That's just the way he is—so unreliable. He went right off to find you and left all the cleaning materials in the middle of the living-room floor!"

The girls laughed and followed Mrs Holman round from place to place to finish Fred's work. By the time the house was tidy, it was midday and they all moved into the kitchen. As they prepared sandwiches and salad for lunch, they talked about the fake phone message.

Mrs Holman, now that her worry was over, became angry. "I think hoaxes are the lowest form of humour. I'd like to find out who played that trick."

George said, "When we solve the mystery, I'm sure we'll find out."

As soon as the group had finished eating, Nancy said she would like to go back to the site of the Indian village. The other girls agreed to go with her.

Once more the three got their digging tools and set off, taking the same route they had followed on their previous trip.

"When we come back, let's try a shortcut," George proposed. "This spade is kind of heavy."

"Good idea," Nancy agreed. "Girls, I've just had a hunch that we're going to find someone else has been digging at the village."

"You mean since we've been there?" George asked.

"Yes, I do. That was the reason for the fake phone call."

This thought spurred the other girls on. As they neared the clearing, Nancy suggested that they go forward cautiously.

"If we do find someone digging," she said, "and can capture him, we may have the phantom right in our grasp!"

"Oh, my goodness!" said Bess. "I don't like capturing criminals!"

George looked disdainful. "What kind of sleuth are you, anyway?"

Bess became silent and she stayed at the rear of the trio, which now proceeded in single file. At the edge of the clearing Nancy held up her hand and put a finger to her lips. She hid behind a tree and motioned the other girls to do so.

"Look!" she whispered.

In the centre of the Indian village were half a dozen deep holes. Nancy's hunch had been right!

Suddenly Bess and George realized that her finger was not pointing at the freshly dug pits, but at the figure of a man disappearing among the trees across from them. He was carrying a spade and running as fast as he could.

"Let's get him!" Nancy urged.

The three girls dropped their tools and took off after the man. He had a head start and ran a zigzag course which put him out of their sight most of the time. They could not see his face, but he was a rather slight man of medium height and had dark, thinning hair. Could he be the one whose footprints Nancy had followed in the woods?

After a while he failed to reappear, but the girls kept running in the direction where they had last seen him. This brought them to the shore of the cove. They looked down the embankment. He was not in sight, but suddenly Bess exclaimed, "There goes a man in a rowing-boat! Isn't he the one?"

The man was rowing hard but in reverse motion, so that his back was towards the girls—apparently to avoid identification.

"I don't see any name or number on the boat," said Nancy. "Do you?"

Neither Bess nor George did. But they felt sure that the way the man was acting proved him to be guilty of something. Was he the one who had phoned the fake message to the Rorick house?"

Nancy heaved a sigh. "If he did find the treasure—which I doubt—we know he didn't carry it with him, unless it was so small he slipped it into a pocket."

George smiled. "Maybe we'll come across a chest of gold that he dropped!"

The girls hurried back to the spot where they had left their digging tools, picked them up, and walked into the Indian village. They checked the holes made by the mysterious digger and found them empty. Then the young sleuths stopped talking and went to work with a will.

Presently George called out that she had found an arrowhead. "This place is probably full of them."

Nancy was more fortunate. About ten minutes later

she unearthed a small pottery idol. It was a bit damaged but recognizable as an Indian god.

She showed it to the others, saying, "I don't know whether I can keep this or not. One thing I never did find out was, who owns this property."

"I did," said George. "The town of Emerson."

"Then anything we dig up will be turned over to the authorities," said Nancy. "That makes it simple."

The digging went on. Bess wandered off some distance to work. After a time Nancy noticed her and was about to call when suddenly Bess gave a cry. It sounded more like fright than surprise.

· 13 ·

The Cave Clue

NANCY and George hurried over to Bess. She was standing in a pit, trembling like a leaf. They were about to ask her what the trouble was when they looked near her feet.

She had unearthed a human skull!

"Gosh!" George exclaimed. "You've dug up a grave!"

"A very old one, I'd say," Nancy put in.

Bess scrambled up out of the pit, but still cringed at the sight of the blankly staring skull. Nancy and George, however, were fascinated.

"I wonder if it's an Indian's skull or someone who died more recently," Nancy mused. "Let's dig some more and see if there's a body."

"If you don't mind," said Bess, "I'll go dig somewhere else for the treasure from the *Lucy Belle*."

The other girls smiled but told her to go ahead. Using their digging tools very carefully, they dug deeper into the pit and in a little while disinterred a whole skeleton.

"It was an Indian all right," said Nancy, as she brushed away dirt from one of its legs, disclosing a beaded anklet.

George surveyed the scene. "I wonder if this person

was buried wearing other jewellery which later was stolen from the body."

Nancy said that judging by the depth of the pit, perhaps George's second guess was right. Whoever had disinterred the Indian the first time had covered it lightly with soil and not bothered to fill in the whole deep grave.

Nancy said excitedly, "I have a feeling we have unearthed something valuable that a museum might be glad to get. I think we should notify the police and suggest that a professor from the university come and look at this skeleton."

"I think you're right," George said.

By this time Bess's courage had returned, and overcome with curiosity, she appeared at the edge of the pit. She was just in time to hear Nancy's suggestion.

"I think your idea is a good one, Nancy. Suppose I go back to the house and phone the police?"

Nancy and George grinned and told her to go ahead. They knew Bess was eager to get away from the gruesome sight.

"While she's gone," Nancy suggested, "let's dig around here a little more. Maybe we can find some of the Indian's possessions."

After ten minutes' work they uncovered a rotting bow and arrow but did not dare pick them up for fear they would disintegrate. Weary now from their digging, the girls sat down to rest and await the police.

Chief Ruskin soon arrived with two professors from the university museum and Bess. The three men stared in astonishment at the girls' find.

Professor Greentree was a newcomer to Emerson and an authority on Indian history.

"I've been planning a dig on this site," he said with a smile. "You girls have beaten me to it." He went to his car for a special stretcher. Then, very carefully, he and his colleague inserted it under the old figure. The fragile skeleton was lightly covered with a piece of gauze and carried to the professor's station wagon which was parked in a side road beyond the clearing.

"I'm glad that's over," said Bess. "And I hope we don't meet any more prehistoric men!"

"Prehistoric?" George repeated. "Why, that skeleton is probably only a couple of hundred years old. Rather handsome, too."

George's cousin ignored the remark. She turned to Nancy. "What do we do now?"

Nancy reminded the girls they had come to hunt for the long-lost wedding gifts. "Let's dig a little longer."

"I'm getting hungry," said Bess as a gentle hint that they should give up. But the others, after glancing at their wrist watches, told her it was nowhere near dinner time yet.

"Promise me we'll go in half an hour," she pleaded.

"Okay," Nancy agreed. "And instead of digging, why don't we just search this area for clues?"

Bess felt better and eagerly joined the search. Weeds were pushed aside, rocks moved out of position.

Presently Nancy said in a low voice, "Listen! I thought I heard someone."

The girls straightened up and looked all around. They could see no one.

Bess was uneasy. "Probably the phantom is spying on us. It gives me the creeps."

"Let's pretend to leave and keep turning round. Maybe we'll spot someone," Nancy suggested.

The girls picked up their tools and started walking towards the cove. Every few minutes they would stop and listen. The crackle of twigs behind them left no doubt but that they were being followed. Yet the spy kept well hidden.

Nancy purposely was taking a zigzag course, not following their usual route. Soon they rounded a low hill and stopped again to listen. There was no sound of pursuit and they walked on. Suddenly they came face to face with a shallow cave.

The girls peered inside. Its stone walls were blackened with smoke. Chest-high was a ledge, evidently man-made with crude tools.

"Do you think Indians used this cave?" Bess asked.

"Here's your answer," said George, as she picked up a tiny flint arrowhead from the mouth of the cave. "This is called a bird point and may have been used for hunting birds."

Nancy walked around, examining the rough stone-work. Above the shelf she noticed an embedded rock that protruded beyond the others. Curious, she tried pulling it out. The stone gave way easily, showing a small niche behind it.

Looking inside, Nancy saw some coloured beads and a piece of ribbon, which she pulled out. The ribbon was black, about an inch wide and very old. On it in tarnished gold letters was the word *Belle*.

Nancy showed it to the others, who gasped.

"A clue!" exclaimed Bess. "This is from the cap of a sailor on the *Lucy Belle*!"

"It must be," said Nancy.

"But how did it get here?" asked Bess.

Nancy had two theories. "Either the sailor left it here, or it fell into the hands of an Indian after the sinking or the massacre. Finding the ribbon here," she added, "lends support to Ben's story." She looked thoughtful. "I wish I knew why the friendly Indians turned on the survivors."

George, who had been standing guard at the entrance to the cave, suddenly hissed, "The spy! I saw him! He looks like the man in the boat!"

"Where is he?" Nancy asked quickly.

Her friend pointed among the trees, but by now the figure had vanished.

"Did he see you?" Nancy asked.

"I don't think so."

This gave Nancy an idea. "What say we surround the spy and capture him?"

To this suggestion, Bess gave a flat veto and no amount of persuasion would make her change her mind. Nancy and George did not think they could carry out the plan alone, so it was abandoned.

Nancy put the ribbon in her pocket and the girls started off once more. This time they could hear footsteps ahead of them in the woods. Once they caught a glimpse of the slight, middle-aged man hurrying away. As the girls quickened their pace, they heard him run. Who was he? Why had he followed them?

Finally they reached the cove at a spot where the embankment was high. Nancy hastened to the edge to see if the mysterious rowboat was anywhere in sight.

As she stood on the brink, suddenly the earth gave way. Nancy struggled to save herself but plunged forward with the rocks and dirt. George tried to grab her friend but failed. She too lost her balance as the earth crumbled still more!

· 14 ·

Puzzling Characters

HORRIFIED, Bess looked down the embankment at the rolling, tumbling girls. She managed to pull back in time to keep from being carried down herself.

"Oh, I hope Nancy and George didn't break any bones!" she thought worriedly.

Both girls had been able to halt their descent just before reaching the little beach. They sat up and clawed dirt from their faces and eyes.

"Are you all right?" Bess called down anxiously.

George looked up at her cousin. "All right, but I'm furious. Why did that earth have to give way just when we were on the trail of the phantom?"

Nancy smiled, despite her dishevelled condition and several scratches. "George, you can make any awful situation seem funny. Just the same, I'm sorry too we lost that man."

The two girls stood up and shook dirt from their clothes. Then, choosing a more solid section of embankment where bushes were growing, they started to climb upward.

Suddenly Bess warned in a hoarse whisper, "Look out there on the water! There's Fred Jenkins in a row-boat!"

Nancy and George turned, but could not see the boat very clearly through the brush. They wondered if Fred had seen them tumble. One thing was sure—he had made no effort to help them. He was far from shore and going past the spot where they were.

As the two girls reached the top of the embankment, Bess said, "The rowboat Fred was in looked just like the one we saw that mysterious man go off in!"

"The boat wasn't marked and there may be many others like it," George said. "Personally, I think Fred Jenkins is too stupid to be mixed up in this mystery."

"Well, I'm not so sure he isn't in it," Nancy declared. "Doesn't it strike you as odd that very often he is around when we are? I admit he seems stupid, but someone else may be having him spy on us. It's even possible he personally faked that telephone call about Hannah Gruen."

George was indignant. "I vote we find out at once."

Bess looked at her cousin and asked, "And how in the world are you going to do that? If Fred is guilty, you don't suppose he's going to tell us?"

George had no answer to this and the three girls walked along in silence for several minutes. Then Nancy said, "I think I have a solution. We'll ask Mrs Holman where Fred lives and quiz some of his neighbours about him."

When they reached home, the housekeeper looked in astonishment at Nancy and George. "You really meant it when you said you were going digging. Did you find anything besides the skeleton?"

Nancy showed her the ribbon with the word *Belle* on it and explained where she had found it. "That's our whole score," said George, "plus some beads and arrowheads. No wedding gifts, no gold."

The girls bathed and put on fresh clothes. They came downstairs and asked Mrs Holman for Fred Jenkins' address. She gave it to them and inquired, "Do you want to see him?"

Nancy told her what she had in mind, but pledged the housekeeper to secrecy. "I won't say a word," the woman promised.

It was late afternoon when the girls set off in the convertible with the top down. Fred lived in a section of old, small homes. The guest house where he had a room was respectable but run down.

A pleasant woman answered Nancy's ring and said that Fred was not at home. She smirked broadly. "*Three* attractive young ladies coming to visit him! And him kind of simple at times."

Bess and George were about to reveal that they were not personal friends of Fred's, but Nancy gave them a warning look. A sudden idea had come to her.

She laughed. "Fred is simple only at times?" she asked the landlady.

"That's right," the garrulous woman replied. "He's as bright as the next one when he sets his mind to it."

"I'm glad to hear that," said Nancy. "Otherwise, it would be hard for him to earn a living, I suppose."

The guest-house owner stared at Nancy. "You're a bright one yourself. You're right. Fred couldn't hold down a job if he wasn't bright sometimes."

Nancy went on quickly. "That's why we're here—to see about giving Fred a job. I want my car washed. But I'll be in touch with him."

The woman assured her that she knew Fred would be delighted to do any kind of a job for such an attractive girl. Nancy ignored the compliment. Secretly she wondered if the woman were trying to get information from her. She asked, "Oh, by the way, does Fred have a family?"

"The only one I know about is his pa. He lives here with Fred."

"I see," said Nancy. "I suppose he's employed too?"

The guest-house owner crossed her arms and leaned forward so that her face was very close to Nancy's. She spoke as if she didn't want anyone to hear her except the girls.

"Kind of funny about him. He's a strange man. Don't talk much, and as far as I know he don't work neither. But you know what? The last month or so, every single clear day he leaves here in the morning and don't come back until night."

"What makes you think he's not working?" Nancy asked.

The woman shrugged. "Oh, you can tell. I've had enough boarders in this place to know when somebody's got a regular job and when they ain't. But I just can't figure out what that man is doing with himself all day."

A silence followed which George broke by grinning and saying, "Maybe he's sitting in the park feeding the birds!"

The woman laughed, but said, "Not him. He's got a gleam in his eye, like he's got something to do. I try to talk to him sometimes, but he always cuts me off."

"Does he look like Fred?" Bess asked.

"No, he's a little fella compared to his son. Fred's

got good muscles. I think one time he did a little boxing." The woman laughed softly. "Maybe he got punched in the head and that's what makes him simple sometimes."

After thanking the landlady for the information, the girls said goodbye. Bess and George noticed that Nancy did not leave her name and address. When they had crossed the street and were back in the convertible, Bess asked her about this. "Did you really mean that about Fred washing your car?"

"You'll admit it could stand a wash and we needed an excuse for coming. The reason I didn't leave my name and address is that I'm sure Fred'll figure out who was asking for him. I'm convinced his stupidity and forgetfulness is an act. He's plenty smart enough to be working against us in this mystery."

"And what about his father?" George asked. "He sounded like a mysterious person. Do you suppose *he* could be the digger?"

Before Nancy could answer, the girls saw a short, slight man walking towards the house.

"He's the man we saw in the rowboat this afternoon!" Bess cried.

He looked at the girls for a second, then turned suddenly and hurried down the street, almost on a run.

"I'll follow him," Nancy said.

This meant turning the car round, which lost precious time. The other girls saw the man turn a corner, but by the time Nancy reached the intersection, he was out of sight.

"Why would he run away unless he's guilty?" Bess mused.

"Good question," George answered. "But guilty of what?"

If Nancy came to any conclusions, she kept them to herself. During the rest of the drive she was silent, preoccupied with her own thoughts. This had certainly been an eventful day.

"But what have I really learned from it?" she asked herself. The mystery seemed as baffling as ever, but she felt sure that the man who had eluded them was mixed up in it somehow. "And he certainly fits the description of Fred's father," she decided.

When the girls reached the Rorick home they found Ned, Burt, and Dave sprawled out in comfortable chairs in the living-room. As they rose to greet the girls, they pretended to be weak-kneed and dizzy. "Oh, all that studying today!" Dave said. "I'm only half-alive!"

The other two boys looked equally exhausted. "But you can help us," Burt said weakly.

"How?" George asked suspiciously.

"By taking pity on us," Ned said. He added, "Just go out into the country with us for dinner and some dancing. You'll be surprised how soon we'll revive."

Everyone laughed. In unison, the three girls said, "We accept."

"Chuck Wilson and his date are coming too," Ned said, "so we rented a large car."

Nancy went to tell Mrs Holman where they were going. The woman said she hoped the young people would have fun. Then Nancy went to her room to put away her car keys.

The evening was wonderful indeed, not only because of the animated conversation, good food, and excellent music, but because of plans Nancy was able to make.

She announced to the others, "Ned and I have made a date to go diving for the *Lucy Belle*!"

"That's good," said Chuck. "What do you hope to find?"

Nancy chuckled. "Treasure!"

Since the boys had to study the following morning, the girls insisted they all return home at a reasonable hour so their escorts could get up early. Ned took the wheel, and after dropping off Chuck and his date, finally turned into the Rorick driveway. The headlights shone brightly on the front of the house.

Suddenly Nancy gasped and exclaimed, "My car is gone!"

· 15 ·

Tell-tale Grass

At Nancy's announcement the six young people jumped from Ned's car and began searching for Nancy's convertible.

"Did you leave the key in the ignition or somewhere else in the car?" Ned asked.

"No, I didn't, Ned. I made a special trip to my room to put the car keys away."

He suggested that Nancy run upstairs and find out if they were still there. In a few minutes she returned, waving her keys. "Here they are. No thief took them."

Bess stated flatly, "The phantom must have stolen the car!"

"Then he's pretty clever at starting a motor without keys," Dave remarked.

"Oh, Nancy, what will you do?" Bess wailed.

Nancy said she would call the police immediately and went into the house. Mrs Holman, extremely nervous over this latest occurrence in the mystery, declared she felt responsible.

"I should have kept my ears open," she said. "But I admit I had the TV on and didn't hear a sound from outside."

"It's not your fault," Nancy said kindly, slipping an arm round the woman's shoulders.

Nancy phoned police headquarters and gave a description of her car, the licence and engine numbers. "I'll alert our men at once," the duty sergeant told her.

A few minutes later Nancy was thanking Ned for the fun-filled evening.

"I'm sorry it had to end this way," he said. "But cheer up! The Emerson police will locate your car, even if they haven't found the phantom!"

Nancy was awakened the next day by a tap on her door and called, "Come in!" Mrs Holman stood there, a broad smile on her face.

"You won't believe it, Nancy, but your car is back!"

"What!" Nancy cried. "The police found it this quickly?"

Mrs Holman said she did not know who had found it. When she had looked out of her bedroom window which faced the front of the house, there stood Nancy's car! "Come and see for yourself!"

Nancy flew into the housekeeper's bedroom and gazed down at her lovely convertible. Impulsively she hugged Mrs Holman. "Isn't this marvellous!"

"It's like a miracle," the woman said.

"I must call the police at once and ask them where they found it," said Nancy.

She hurried into Mr Rorick's bedroom and dialled the number. Chief Rankin answered the phone. As the girl bubbled over with thanks at the prompt police action, he broke in, saying, "Miss Drew, I'm as amazed as you are to learn that the car is back. My men did not pick it up."

"They didn't!" Nancy exclaimed unbelievingly.

"That's right. When the night patrol went off duty, they reported no luck. And none of the day men have called in yet."

Nancy said if she learned the answer to this puzzle, she would let the chief know. She hung up, went back to her room to dress quickly, then sped downstairs and outdoors.

Curious, she looked first at the ignition lock. There was no key in it! Nancy blinked. "If I hadn't had witnesses," she thought, "I'd think I had dreamed the whole thing!"

Now Nancy noticed that the car had been washed and polished! Instantly her mind flew to Fred Jenkins. Had the guest-house owner told him what Nancy had said? Did *he* know how to start a car without a key?

"But this is crazy! If Fred knew I wanted him to wash the car, why didn't he just come here today and do it?"

Nancy strode back into the house. By this time Bess and George were up. They were amazed to hear what had happened. Bess shook her head in complete puzzlement. "Nancy, this is the craziest mystery you've ever asked us to help you solve!"

Nancy laughed. "I guess you're right."

After breakfast Fred Jenkins arrived to cut the grass on the front lawn. She rushed outside and asked him point-blank, "Fred, did you take my car away from here last night and wash it?"

The youth, instead of being startled, grinned. "Yes, Miss Nancy, I did. Guess you were surprised."

"Surprised!" exclaimed Nancy. "I was greatly alarmed. Why did you do it?"

Fred looked at her as if he were hurt. "You wanted your car washed, didn't you?"

Nancy stared at the young man. "But how did you move it? I didn't leave the key in it!"

Fred looked blank. "Yes, you did, Miss Nancy. Otherwise, I couldn't have started it."

The two stared at each other, deadlocked on the subject. Nancy had a strong hunch Fred was lying. But what was the point of it all?

Fred looked around uneasily and said in a low voice, "You say you didn't leave the key in the lock, but still I found one. Besides, I left it there. That's kind of spooky, isn't it?"

Nancy eyed him thoughtfully. "It's gone now," she said, then asked, "How much do I owe you for washing the car?"

Fred answered loftily. "I wouldn't think of taking any money. It was a pleasure to do something for you and I'm sorry I frightened you."

"That's all right," Nancy said, smiling warmly. "Thank you so much."

Later, when she was talking to the other girls about the strange episode, George said, "Don't let him fool you, Nancy. He meant to steal the car, but somehow he heard the police had been alerted, so he washed it to have an alibi, and brought it back."

Bess was sure George was right. Nancy did not commit herself. She changed the subject and said, "Let's investigate the library and see if the phantom has been here again. Last time I was in there I switched two books with the word *roar* in them. I'll be curious to see if they're still where I left them."

Suddenly Bess giggled. "Poor Uncle John! He'll never know where to find his books again. They've been put back helter-skelter."

Nothing in the library looked as if it had been disturbed since the girls' last visit, but the two books Nancy had mentioned had been put back in their places.

"Well," said Bess, "if the phantom has been here again, he wasn't so disorderly this time."

Mrs Holman, who had followed the girls into the room, heard the remark and a look of fright came over her face.

Nancy turned to her. "Mrs Holman, have you been in this room since all of us were here together."

"No indeed. I wouldn't come in alone if I were paid to do so!"

"But somebody with bits of grass on his shoes has been," Nancy stated.

The others looked at her blankly. "How do you know?" the housekeeper asked.

The young sleuth pointed towards the safe. In front of it was a sprinkling of shrivelled-up grass clippings. There were no footprints to be seen, but Nancy rushed upstairs for her special magnifying glass and went over the carpet in front of the safe. She could find no prints. There were none anywhere else in the room except those made by Mrs Holman and the girls.

Nancy continued to stare at the bits of grass. "Fred mowed the back lawn yesterday," she said, "so the phantom must have come through it last night. These cuttings are withered."

"He got into the house through locked doors again," Mrs Holman said grimly.

Nancy decided to try once more to find an opening into the room. She would see if any of the built-in book-cases moved outwards and perhaps reveal a secret entrance to the library. She asked the others to help her and together they tugged and hunted for hidden springs. They could find nothing.

Presently Mrs Holman announced that she would have to be excused to get luncheon. She expected Mr Rorick home by one o'clock. Bess offered to help her while Nancy and George continued to search.

"How do you figure anyone can walk around here without leaving footprints?" George questioned.

Nancy shrugged. "I presume he's in stocking-feet. Let's look around outdoors and see if we can find any evidence."

Nancy locked the library door and the two girls went outside.

"Let's check the grass of the rear lawn first," Nancy suggested.

They found small mounts of withered grass clippings cut by Fred, raked up but not carried away. One pile was partly scattered.

"I guess this is our answer," Nancy said. "The phantom crossed the lawn here, and some clippings clung to the bottom of his trousers. They dropped off while he was kneeling at the safe."

Very faint depressions were visible in the pile—not clear enough to be identified as anyone's footprints. The girls could find nothing else, so now they began to scan the entire foundation carefully. There was not a single footprint near it. Finally the two searchers gave up and went into the house.

At exactly one o'clock Mr Rorick drove up and came in. He was jovial and looked rested from his vacation.

"Well, how's the mystery going?" he asked. "Have you solved it yet?"

Nancy admitted defeat, saying she really was baffled about the phantom. Uncle John praised her for what she had discovered so far and insisted she continue.

"I don't care if it takes all summer," he said. "But just don't leave me with an unsolved mystery."

"All summer!" Nancy instantly thought of all the plans she had and knew she would not be able to stay at Emerson much longer. She set her jaw in determination. Before she left, she *must* find out who the phantom was and how he entered the library!

As soon as luncheon was over, she told Mr Rorick about the pieces of grass in front of the safe. "Perhaps you'd better open the safe and see if everything is still there."

"I'll do that. But it would take a professional safe-cracker to figure out that combination."

The whole group trooped into the library. Mr Rorick knelt on the floor in front of the safe and began to dial the combination. In a few moments he grasped the handle and turned it. The door swung wide open.

Uncle John looked inside. A startled expression came over his face and he quickly began pulling out various envelopes. When they all lay on the floor, he turned to the others, his face pale.

"All the money that was in there is gone!"

· 16 ·

Stolen Coin Collection

"ALL your money's gone!" Bess exclaimed in dismay.

The other girls expressed their sympathy and George suggested calling the police at once.

The elderly man shook his head. "They wouldn't believe us about the phantom, so why should they believe me now?"

The housekeeper asked gently, "Isn't it possible that you took the money out so you'd have it for your trip to the reunion?"

Uncle John Rorick shook his head vigorously. "No," he said. Suddenly the memory of something came to him and he jumped up, his eyes staring into space and his hands clutched above his head. He began to pace the room, shaking his head from side to side as if in great pain.

"Is something else wrong?" Nancy asked.

Mr Rorick turned and faced the others. "My coin collection is gone too!"

At this announcement Mrs Holman fell into a chair. "Your coin collection! Oh no!"

There was silence for several seconds, then Bess ventured, "Was it very valuable?"

"Valuable?" Uncle John almost roared. "It was priceless!"

This statement stunned the girls.

"How were the coins kept?" Nancy asked.

"In collectors' books. They ranged all the way from pennies up to ten-dollar gold pieces in old American money. And then, there were some very rare ones from Europe. I even had some that were minted before Christ. One was a rarity among ancient coins. It contained a female head and had been minted about 350 B.C. in Carthage. The other, showing eagles attacking a hare, was made in 410 B.C. in Agrigentum."

The distraught man continued to walk up and down. Nancy asked him if he had a list of the stolen coins. Mr Rorick shook his head sadly.

"I should have. But I never made one."

"Let's write down as many of them as you can remember," Nancy suggested, "and we can give these to the police at least. You won't refuse now to tell the authorities, will you?"

"No. They should know. I want that collection back! It's worth a fortune!"

As George went to call Chief Rankin, Nancy took a pad and pencil from the desk. She wondered if the thief thought he had found part of the treasure of coins from the *Lucy Belle*.

Nancy began to write as Uncle John dictated. "One of my ten-dollar gold pieces was minted in 1798," he said. "It was in very fine condition and is worth nineteen hundred dollars."

"Nineteen hundred dollars!" Bess repeated.

"Yes," replied Uncle John. "Then there was a half eagle, minted in 1827, that had never been circulated. That's worth twenty-five hundred dollars!"

"Good grief!" George exclaimed.

After a few more minutes of dictating, Uncle John paused. Bess asked him, "What was the most valuable coin in the collection?"

Before he answered, the girls thought they detected tears in the corners of the elderly man's eyes. "It was a gold one-hundred ducat from Poland, dated 1621. On the obverse side is a picture of Sigismund III wearing armour and the collar of the Golden Fleece. On the reverse side there is a crowned shield. It is a real rarity among European coins."

"How much is that worth?" Nancy asked.

"Seventy-five hundred dollars!"

There was a great gasp from the girls and Mrs Holman. All of them came forward either to pat Mr Rorick's shoulder or put an arm round him.

"This is terrible, terrible!" said the housekeeper, who was fighting back tears.

The sad scene was interrupted by the doorbell. Mrs Holman went to answer it and reappeared bringing Chief Rankin with an officer whom he introduced as Detective Newmark.

For the first time the chief admitted that a real phantom thief was plaguing Mr Rorick. The officer expressed regret that there was not a complete list of the coins but took the paper on which Nancy had been writing. When he saw the amounts listed, his eyes widened in amazement.

Detective Newmark examined the bits of grass in front of the safe. Nancy told him how she believed they had been left there, and he thought she was right. Then he asked Mr Rorick if the combination of the safe had been written down and hidden anywhere in the house.

The elderly man shook his head. "My housekeeper and I memorized it. No one else knows the combination and there is no written copy of it."

The two officers gave Mrs Holman a searching look. Mr Rorick came to her defence at once. "Mrs Holman is like a member of my own family. I would trust her with any secret."

"Perhaps," Nancy said, "the theft was done by an expert safecracker."

"That's a possibility," the detective agreed.

"Then the thief is probably an ex-convict or a wanted criminal," the young sleuth suggested.

Chief Rankin admitted this might be the case and asked Detective Newmark to get his finger-printing materials from the car. The detective did this, and went all over the outside and inside of the safe. There was only one set of prints.

"They must be mine," Uncle John spoke up.

The detective got another kit from the car, took the old man's prints, and compared them with the ones he had lifted from the safe. "Yes, Mr Rorick is correct," he said. "Whoever the thief was, he left no finger prints."

Suddenly Mrs Holman gave a tremendous sigh. "Our phantom has no fingerprints and no footprints, and he goes right through the walls!"

Neither of the officers had an answer to the puzzles, but they promised to telephone Mr Rorick if they picked up any professional safe-crackers.

After they had gone, the girls tried once more to comfort their host. Nancy remarked, "Since we can't locate the phantom here, perhaps we can trace the coins and they, in turn, may lead us to the thief."

Mr Rorick sighed. "I'm going to lie down in my room," he said. "Don't anyone disturb me until dinnertime."

Nancy glanced at the desk clock and remarked that she had a date with Ned to go scuba diving. She excused herself and went upstairs. She put on her swimsuit and slipped a dress over it.

Bess and George came to tell her that Burt and Dave had arrived at the house. At the boys' request, they made tentative plans for the three couples to meet at dinnertime.

Ned arrived later. As he and Nancy left, Mrs Holman, on her way to the kitchen, warned the young detective to be careful.

Nancy smiled. "That's just what our housekeeper, Hannah Gruen, would have told me," she said. "Thank you. I promise."

As Ned started the convertible Nancy asked if he would first drive her to the locksmith shops in Emerson. "I want to find out if Fred Jenkins or anybody else had a key made for my car."

She told how Fred had insisted there was a key in the ignition when he had taken the convertible.

"I don't believe that," Ned stated firmly. "But we'll go to the shops and find out."

There were only two locksmiths in town and both of them told Nancy they had not made a car key for Fred Jenkins or any other person during the past two days.

"Just as I suspected!" Nancy exclaimed as Ned drove towards Settlers' Cove. "Fred lied to me and I think I know why."

"Then you're a marvel." Ned grinned.

"He took the car to make me believe that the key had been in it. Then he suggested my key had been two places at once—that there was something supernatural about the incident. He was trying to scare me."

"But why," said Ned, "unless he's mixed up with the phantom?"

"I wouldn't be surprised if he is," Nancy declared.

They discussed the handy-man until they reached the end of the dirt road that led to the riverbank.

"We'd better forget Fred and concentrate on our diving," Ned remarked. "I'm as curious as you to get a glimpse of the *Lucy Belle*."

As the couple were donning their scuba gear, Burt and Dave were talking with Bess and George in the Rorick living-room.

"Where would you like to go?" Burt asked.

George grinned. "Somewhere that won't cost you a nickel."

"Swell!" the boys said in unison.

Becoming serious, George said that she and Bess would like to do something to help Nancy with the mystery. The two couples talked for a long time but came to no conclusion.

Then suddenly Dave said, "Say, maybe that phantom goes down the chimney like Santa Claus!"

Eager for action, the four ran up to the second floor and climbed out of a window on to the roof. They turned towards the chimney which led down to the dining-room and library.

"Look!" said Burt. "There's an iron ladder built on the side of the chimney. Maybe the phantom climbs up that."

Dave offered to climb it. "I'll play Santa!" he said.

Reaching the top, he looked inside. Apparently he saw something interesting, because he leaned far down. The next instant his feet slipped off the top rung of the ladder. Dave disappeared head first down the chimney!

· 17 ·

Scuba Scare

"OH!" Bess screamed in fright as she saw Dave fall.

She dashed across the roof and climbed the ladder. Looking into the chimney, she could see Dave's legs thrashing wildly. He was not far down.

"Are you hurt?" she called to him anxiously. His reply was a muffled, unintelligible one.

George and Burt had hurried to the foot of the chimney and wanted to know what had happened.

"Dave's stuck, but I think we can pull him out," Bess answered. "Climb up here and we'll try."

The two quickly climbed the ladder. Burt grabbed one of Dave's legs, while the two girls took the other. It was a precarious position for George and Burt, since Bess was the only one with a good foothold. In trying to yank out their friend, George and Burt might easily lose their balance.

"Be careful!" Bess warned them. "One accident is enough."

Dave seemed to be pinned in such a way that he was unable to help himself. George guessed that probably his head and shoulders were stuck in one of the flues. The imprisoned boy began to cough. No doubt he was breathing soot!

"Let's pull!" Burt urged. "One, two, three!"

He and the two girls tugged with all their might and managed to move Dave's body upwards about six inches. There were more muffled words from him, but this time Bess was sure he was saying, "Take it easy!"

Burt called down, "Hold your breath, buddy. It will make it easier for us!"

He now asked the girls to give another yank. This time Dave was able to call out clearly, "Okay," and began to help himself.

Little by little he was pulled to the top of the chimney. What a sight he was—completely blackened with soot! But Dave seemed unhurt as he perched on the edge of the chimney.

"You sure you're all right?" Bess asked solicitously.

"Sure," said Dave. "But give me first prize for being the stupidest guy in Emerson!"

Burt grinned. "And the dirtiest! You look like the black Phantom!"

Everyone laughed, then George asked if Dave had found out anything by his descent.

"Only that there are two flues that go off at angles. As a detective, I'm afraid I'm a failure. What do you say we all go into the house? I'd like to take a shower."

Bess climbed down the ladder, went across the roof, and through the attic window. The others followed in quick succession. When they reached the first floor, Bess suggested that Burt bring down Dave's sooty clothes which could be put through the washing machine and the drier.

"I'll do that," he said.

The girls found Mrs Holman in the kitchen and

explained what had happened. She shook her head and said, "I never knew people could have so many adventures in such a short time!"

Bess laughed. "This is one we can't blame on Nancy except indirectly."

George noticed a large, shopping-order pad and a pencil hanging on a hook. She removed them and began to sketch. Mrs Holman and Bess were busy talking about what had happened to Dave and did not notice the picture George was drawing.

A moment later Burt appeared with the sooty clothes and Bess asked if she might use the washer and drier.

"Yes, indeed," said Mrs Holman. "I'll go down to the basement with you and show you how they work. Afterwards, I'll press the suit for you."

While the two were gone, George continued her work. Twenty minutes later it was finished, and even she as creator had to smile at it. The sketch showed a chimney with a ladder. Diving into it head first was Santa Claus. Underneath she had printed: SANTA CLAUS GOES TO MEET THE PHANTOM.

When the whole group assembled later, she presented the picture to Dave. He roared with laughter and passed it round.

Then he said, "Santa Claus always leaves gifts. Tell you what. I'll take you all to supper if you'll pick out a place that won't empty my pockets."

George laughed. "We won't give you a chance to change your mind!"

The four young people left the house, telling Mrs Holman where they would be, in case Nancy and Ned should inquire.

At that moment the young sleuth and her companion were deep in the water. They had been swimming for some time, searching the murky bottom with the lights on their headgear. Suddenly Nancy's heart began to pound with excitement. Below them was a large hulk. The *Lucy Belle*! It was indeed sunken in a watery valley and partially covered with weeds and silt.

Nancy swam round the deck, trying to locate hatches. Not seeing any, she stood on the deck to look into the cabin.

Without warning the rotted wood below her suddenly gave way, and before Nancy could make motions to swim upwards, she fell through. Her tank hose became tangled in the broken timbers and in a moment her supply of oxygen was cut off!

Like a flash Ned was at her side. He gently pulled her upwards and straightened out the hose. She nodded her thanks. The fright had left Nancy feeling a bit weak and Ned led her away from the danger spot.

He motioned as if to say, "We'd better go up!"

But as soon as Nancy had taken a few deep breaths, she felt stronger. She pointed towards the hold of the ship and started swimming round it, hoping to find an opening.

"I want to investigate the hold," she indicated to Ned.

On the far side of the sunken vessel they found a huge hole where a hatch had evidently blown out. Apparently this was where cargo had been loaded and unloaded.

With their headgear lights turned on full, the two swimmers went inside. As they had expected, they were in the engine room where the fatal explosion had taken place. They swam through blown-out walls into the area beyond. There was no question but that this was the hold of the ship. However, there was nothing in it. They both wondered what had happened to the contents.

Ned was thinking, "Probably divers in recent years have taken whatever was here."

Nancy had the same thought, but she still had a strong hunch that the chest of gold coins and the valuable Rorick cargo had been removed from the sinking ship by one or more persons who had escaped the wreck.

The couple swam out of the hold and once more Ned pointed upwards. Again Nancy shook her head. It had occurred to her that possibly the water in the tributary was higher now than it had been back in the 1700's. There might be caves along the coast where the chests had been hidden for safe keeping.

"If something happened to the survivors before they had a chance to come back for the treasure," Nancy reasoned, "then it could still be here!"

She led the way towards the shoreline and began swimming quickly, searching for caves. There was nothing in sight. Finally Ned, indicating that their time for safety underwater was up, insisted that they surface.

In a few moments they came up at a spot not far from where they had parked the car. They removed their scuba gear and sat down in the warm, late-afternoon sun to dry off.

"I'm disgusted," said Nancy. "I didn't learn a thing."

Ned laughed. "You surprise me, Miss Detective. You've always taught me that false clues *do* prove certain things."

The young sleuth smiled. "I stand corrected. We know that the treasures we're looking for are not in the *Lucy Belle* or hidden underwater along this shore."

As soon as the couple had dried off, they walked back to the car. Nancy slipped her dress over her head and put on her sandals while Ned donned shirt and trousers.

He glanced at the car clock and reminded Nancy that it was nearly dinner-time. "Weren't we going to meet the other four?" he asked.

"Yes, if we could make it. But before we go back to the house, I'd like to drive to police headquarters and find out if they've picked up any safecrackers."

When they reached the police building, Nancy hurried inside. The chief was not there but a sergeant on duty answered her question. Two known safecrackers, now on parole, had been picked up for questioning. Both were tall men. They did not fit the description of the phantom thief.

"Thank you," Nancy said. When she reached the car, she relayed the message to Ned. "I have been suspecting a short, slight man of being the phantom. Now the question is, am I wrong or is the phantom someone who does not have a police record?"

Ned chuckled. "Nancy, you certainly can pose the most unanswerable questions. I plead ignorance."

He started the car, but had gone no farther than the next corner when Nancy said, "Please turn left."

"But why?" Ned asked. "We go the other way to Uncle John's."

Nancy explained that it was only a short distance to the guest house where Fred Jenkins lived. "I suspect he's involved in this case, not as the thief necessarily, but in some way is connected with the mystery. We might just happen to be able to learn something."

Ned turned left and Nancy directed him to the street where Fred lived. As they neared his house, Nancy suddenly exclaimed, "Here he comes out the door! And look who's with him! The man that Bess and George and I have caught glimpses of in the woods. We think *he* may be the phantom!"

"But who is he?" Ned asked.

"I believe he's Fred's father. Oh, Ned, maybe we're going to learn something really worthwhile! Let's follow them!"

· 18 ·

Secret Key Maker

FRED JENKINS and the man with him proved to be fast walkers. They apparently were in a hurry to get somewhere and did not turn once, so Nancy felt sure that they had not spotted her car following them.

After walking two blocks the men went into a garage. Ned parked some distance down the street and they waited. Soon a battered old car was driven out of the building by Fred Jenkins. The slight man sat beside him.

"Let's go!" Nancy urged. "But try to keep at least two cars behind them."

The trail led a good distance out into the country. As Ned watched the road, Nancy kept her eyes on Fred and the other man. So far as she could judge, they took no particular notice of the couple. Presently the men turned left on a narrow dirt lane which led towards the river.

"Shall I still follow?" Ned asked, stopping at the turnoff.

"Not with the car," Nancy replied. "How about parking it over there among the trees? Then we'll follow on foot."

"Okay."

After Ned had put the top up, locked the car, and pocketed the keys, the couple started down the lane. There had been no rain for several days and the roadway was extremely dusty. The tyre tracks of Fred Jenkins' car were easy to see.

Nancy walked in the grass along the side, explaining that it was less dusty and also it might be just as well if the two of them did not leave footprints.

The lane was long, and as they came near the river, there were trees on both sides. They were so close together that it was difficult to see anything beyond them.

Suddenly Nancy stopped short. "I hear a car. It sounds as if it's going from the river in the direction of the main road."

"Do you think Fred left his passenger at the river front and has taken another lane back?"

Nancy shrugged, but quickened her step. A few minutes later she and Ned could see the water. The lane turned right and ended in a small clearing where a ramshackle cabin stood. Fred's car was nowhere in sight.

"He went that way," Nancy said, pointing to a field of tall grass beyond the shack. A wide track of broken weeds showed where the car had been driven into it.

"They must have spotted us," Ned remarked, "or they'd have gone back up the lane."

"I wonder if they had business at this cabin," Nancy pondered.

As she started towards it, Ned caught her arm. "Better let me go first."

He knocked on the door. There was no answer.

After several knocks the couple concluded the cabin was vacant. Ned tried the door, which opened easily. There was only one large room and no one was in it.

"You stand guard at the door, Nancy," Ned suggested. "I'll just take a look around to see if I can pick up any clues."

Nancy looked out at the lane and the field, then turned to see what progress Ned was making. He was opening cupboards. All proved to be bare. Ned began to sing out:

> *"Snoopy Ned Nickerson went to the cupboard*
> *To find Nancy Drew a clue.*
> *But when he got there,*
> *Each cupboard was bare*
> *And so there was no clue for Drew."*

Nancy laughed heartily. She was about to remark that perhaps they had better go, when Ned slid back a panel under the sink. Forgetting that Nancy was standing guard, he cried out, "Nancy, look at this!"

She darted across the room as he began dragging out a heavy machine. Nancy stared at it in utter astonishment.

"It's a key-making machine!"

"It sure is," said Ned. He reached farther back under the sink. "And here are boxes and boxes of blanks. This is a locksmith's secret workshop!"

"And I suspect," Nancy said, "that the locksmith is Fred Jenkins' father! If I'm right, he could make keys to open many locks."

Ned looked at her. "Are you trying to say that he

opens any door he wishes to in the Rorick house? In other words, he's the phantom thief?"

"I have a strong hunch he is," Nancy replied.

"In that case," Ned said, "I think we should take this machine and the blanks to the police and you should report your suspicions to them."

"I agree about taking the machine to the police, but I haven't a shred of evidence that Fred or his father have anything to do with it." She decided not to mention their names until she had proof of their guilt.

Since the key-making machine was heavy, Ned said he would bring the car down. He asked Nancy to keep out of sight behind some trees in case the men returned. No one came, however, and in a little while the machine and the blanks were loaded into the car.

Ned drove at once to police headquarters. Chief Rankin, on duty now, was very much interested in the couple's story, and was glad they had brought in the machine. "I'll have some of my men watch the cabin to see who goes there."

As Nancy and Ned finally drove towards the Rorick house, Nancy had an idea. "Are any ironmongeries open this late?" she asked.

"One is. What's on your mind?"

"I was just thinking," said Nancy, "that if the key-making machine we found belongs to the phantom, he won't be able to make any more. So if we put a new padlock on the library door, he can't get in there!"

"That's right," Ned agreed, and turned down a side street to an ironmonger's. The new padlock was purchased, this one with an alarm on it, then the couple left.

When they reached the Rorick home, Mrs Holman told them where the other young people had gone. She and Uncle John were just about to sit down to dinner and asked the young couple to eat with them. "Then you can tell us all that has happened," the housekeeper said.

Smiling, Ned sniffed the air and said, "I smell roast beef! How could we refuse?"

The others laughed. A few minutes later the four sat down at the table. Nancy and Ned both laughed and shuddered upon hearing the story of Dave's fall into the chimney. Then they related all of their adventures and why they had bought a new padlock.

"This is a brand-new type," Ned said, showing how it worked. "The man told us they had just come in and his store is the only one in Emerson to stock them."

"It has an alarm on it," Nancy explained. "If anyone tries to pick it tonight we'll certainly know it!"

"Very good," said Mr Rorick.

Mrs Holman added, "I'm sure I'll sleep better now."

Nancy said that she had a plan to put into operation after dinner. It would prove whether or not the phantom did enter the library by way of the door.

"Uncle John, would you mind going in there as soon as it's dark and turning on all the lights? Don't draw the curtains. Take all the notes from your wallet and place them in a couple of the books with the word *roar* in them. Be sure to put them on the pages which match the amount of money."

Uncle John smiled. "You want to trap the phantom?"

Nancy laughed. "That's right. If he's watching, I'm sure he won't be able to resist the money."

Mrs Holman remarked, "It's deliberately inviting a burglar into your home. But I suppose it's worth the risk if it will trap the thief."

About ten o'clock Bess and George and their dates arrived and the whole group talked for some time. Uncle John had played his role of planting the money in the library, the old padlocks had been removed and the new one installed. Everyone felt sure the mystery was about to be solved. Ned, Burt, and Dave offered to keep watch, but Mr Rorick insisted that he could handle the situation.

The boys left at eleven o'clock. Windows and doors were securely locked, then Uncle John, Mrs Holman, and the three girls went to the first floor.

Bess and George soon fell asleep, but Nancy was restless. She kept getting out of bed and walking to the window. About twelve o'clock, as she gazed towards the woods, she saw a flickering light spring up among the trees.

"The phantom is here!" she murmured to herself.

She watched for some time, then the light went out. Was the mysterious person on his way to the house? Would he soon let himself in and find the new padlock? Nancy tensed, waiting for the alarm to sound.

The minutes crept by. All was silent. Nancy began to feel chilly and went back to bed. She listened intently but could hear nothing downstairs. Finally, in sheer exhaustion, she fell asleep.

In the morning everyone compared notes. No one had heard the alarm go off!

"But how about the money in the library?" Mrs Holman asked. "If it has been stolen, then we'll know that the thief *is* a phantom and goes through walls!" But the others were certain that the money would still be in the books.

The group watched while Nancy opened the padlock, then they marched into the library. Everyone waited excitedly while Mr Rorick went to examine the hiding places in the books.

He picked up one and looked inside. A peculiar expression came over his face. He did not speak. Instead, he turned the book upside down and shook it. No money fluttered out!

·19·

An Amazing Passageway

THE whole affair took an unexpected turn. Nancy went up to Mrs Holman and hugged her.

"You were right all along. The phantom literally goes 'through the walls'."

"Oh, bless you!" the housekeeper said, tears in her eyes. "I'm glad that someone believes me."

George, always practical, asked, "But which wall?"

Mr Rorick stood stupefied. He seemed completely unable to believe what had happened. Again the phantom had taken his money without any visible means of entrance and exit. The elderly man shook his head in dismay.

Finally Nancy answered George's question. "As you know, I have searched this room thoroughly, and the police have, too. There's one place left that the thief may use—a spot I thought was impossible."

"What's that?" Bess asked.

"The chimney."

"But how could the phantom get through solid brick?" Bess argued.

George snapped her fingers. "When we were up on the roof, Dave said the flues slanted towards the outside of the chimney. Could that have anything to do with it?"

"It certainly could," Nancy replied. "I wish I'd known this before."

She looked up the flue in the library, then dashed out to the hall and into the dining-room. In a few moments she was back.

"The flues are far apart from left to right as you stand in front of this fireplace," she reported. "I wonder if, by any chance, there could be an opening between them which runs from here into the dining-room!"

Everyone gazed at the wooden panelling which covered the fireplace wall from ceiling to mantel. For the first time Nancy realized that the mantelshelf was very wide—wide enough for a person to stand on. Grabbing the shelf with both hands, she pulled herself up and began tapping each panel. Suddenly a broad smile lighted up her face.

"There's a small section here that sounds hollow!" she exclaimed.

Nancy hunted a long time for a hidden spring. She pushed on various sections of each panel and also tried to raise or slide them. But she failed to detect anything which might open a hidden door. The young sleuth refused to give up.

Although the panels were tightly wedged together, Nancy was sure there was some mechanism hidden between two of them.

"Bess, will you find me the thinnest nail file you can?" she requested.

In less than a minute Bess was back with an almost paper-thin one. Carefully Nancy tried inserting it between a hollow-sounding panel and the one next to it.

Suddenly her efforts were rewarded. The nail file pressed out a wafer-thin metal lever and at the same moment the whole section above the centre of the fireplace swung outwards. It swept Nancy to the floor!

"You've done it! You've found it!" Bess cried ecstatically as she helped Nancy to her feet.

The whole group gazed into a dark, narrow passageway which they felt sure opened into the dining-room.

"We'll find out in a minute!" Nancy said, running from the room. The others followed.

Nancy removed the candlesticks from the dining-room mantelshelf. Then she climbed up and inserted the nail file in the section that backed up the one above the fireplace in the library. A long, narrow door, reaching from the ceiling to the shelf, opened outwards.

Mr Rorick was flabbergasted. "This is one secret which was never passed down in the family," he declared.

"But someone else learned about it," said George. "Yippee! Nancy has solved the mystery of the phantom! He climbed through the passageway from the dining-room, did his thieving and searching, then climbed up, closed the secret door behind him, and let himself out here."

Mrs Holman, who had been speechless all this time, now found her voice. "The police should be notified at once and come here to catch that criminal!"

Before anyone else could answer her, Nancy said, "Oh, please don't do that. I want to catch him myself —not just to capture him, but to see if I can find out what else he has been searching for."

She looked pleadingly at Mr Rorick. Finally he said, "I think we owe it to Nancy Drew to let her have her way. But there must be restrictions and a time limit. Don't take any chances. And if you don't capture him by tomorrow, then I feel I ought to notify the authorities."

Nancy was ready to put a plan into action at once. "When will Fred be here again working in the house?" she asked Mrs Holman.

"I expect him early this afternoon."

Nancy smiled. "That will be perfect."

She suggested that after Fred arrived, the others were to talk about two subjects: first, that Mrs Holman and Mr Rorick would be gone for the afternoon, and that the three girls would drive out into the country and not return for several hours. The other was for Uncle John to announce loudly that he had brought some valuable jewellery back with him and would lock it in the safe before leaving.

"If Fred is helping his father or someone else, he'll immediately pass the word along. I'm sure that either he or a confederate will come into the library to take the jewellery."

She went on to say that Mrs Holman was to telephone the house at a certain time and ask Fred to carry a large amount of rubbish out to a certain place in the woods. While he was gone, the three girls would sneak back, go through the secret passageway, and hide themselves behind the sofa and chairs in the library.

Uncle John thought a few moments before giving his consent to the plan. "I suppose it won't be dangerous with three girls against one small man!"

Nancy and her friends smiled. George, to show her enthusiasm, said, "I'm going to make a trial trip through that passageway."

She pulled herself to the mantelshelf and started inside. She was forced to crouch a bit. Suddenly George gave a whoop of elation.

"Uncle John, I've found your coin collection!"

She appeared at the opening to the dining-room, carrying several large coin collectors' books. George handed them down to Mr Rorick, who kept murmuring, "I can't believe it! I can't believe it!"

George went on, "I wonder why the thief didn't take these along with him."

Nancy ventured an answer. "Probably he was afraid to carry them to his home. They're pretty large to conceal. Anyway, he wouldn't dare dispose of many coins at a time and what better hiding place could he have than this passage? By the way, Uncle John, can you tell at a quick glance how much has been taken out?"

Mr Rorick quickly turned the pages of the various books, then smiled in relief. "The thief took only a few hundred dollars' worth. The most valuable coins are still intact. I suppose I was foolish leaving them here, but I like to take the coins out once in a while and look at them."

"But shouldn't you put them in a safe-deposit box now?" Bess asked.

Nancy spoke up. "Why don't we leave them here where the thief hid them? Otherwise, he'll know that the secret passageway has been uncovered and he won't even come into the library!"

Mr Rorick agreed, and George replaced the books where she had found them.

Mrs Holman glanced nervously at her watch. "Sometimes Fred comes early. We'd better close these doors and busy ourselves with some kind of work so he won't be suspicious."

Fred arrived while the group was eating lunch. Mrs Holman asked him to dust the hall where she knew he would overhear everything that was said. The afternoon plans were discussed.

Soon afterwards, everybody in the house except Fred prepared to leave. At two o'clock all had left, and Mrs Holman telephoned Fred at two-thirty. By this time Nancy, Bess, and George had sneaked back to the Rorick home and hidden behind some shrubbery. When they saw Fred carrying the rubbish to the woods, they dashed inside the house. By three o'clock the girls had gone through the secret passageway, closing both the openings, and secreted themselves behind furniture in the library.

They never took their eyes off the chimney. At exactly three-thirty the secret door began to open. A man appeared in the opening and jumped down. He was Fred Jenkins' slightly built companion. The man wore gloves and was in his stocking-feet.

"No wonder he never left any fingerprints or footmarks here," Nancy thought.

The intruder went directly to the safe, knelt down, and slowly turned the dial back and forth. Then he swung the door open, grabbed the velvet case containing costume jewellery which Mr Rorick had put there, closed the safe, and started for the fireplace.

"He's not going to search this time!" Nancy thought. "If we don't capture him now he may get away and take the coin collection with him!"

Quick as a panther Nancy came from behind the sofa and made a leap for the thief. "You're the phantom! Hands up!" she cried. Nancy was counting on the fact that the thief would not turn round and discover that she had no weapon.

Instead of complying, the man whipped a spray gun from his pocket and squirted it into Nancy's face. Instantly she dropped unconscious and he leaped for the mantel.

As George tried to block his way, he turned and gave her a dose of the knockout spray. She too blacked out and fell to the floor. Swiftly the man climbed on to the mantel.

Bess had looked on horrified. If she tried to stop him, no doubt he would give her the same treatment. Then she could not help her friends.

"Oh, what shall I do?" Bess thought with a panicky feeling.

· 20 ·

The Restored Treasure

Bess Marvin quickly collected her wits. She stood up and cried, "Stop!" At the same time, she picked up a heavy book-end from the desk.

As the thief turned to give her a dose from the spray gun, she hurled the book-end directly at it and knocked the weapon from his hand.

The sudden move made the man sway in his precarious position on the mantelshelf. The next instant he lost his balance completely and dropped to the floor. He hit his head hard and lay still.

Instantly Bess pulled herself up to the shelf and darted through the secret passageway. Though her legs were shaking with fright, she ran to the hall telephone.

Picking it up, she dialled the operator and exclaimed, "Send the police to Mr John Rorick's house at once! And have them bring a doctor! There's a thief here and three people have been knocked out!"

She heard a gasp on the other end of the wire but quickly hung up so that no time would be lost in having the message transferred. Bess sat still, trembling like a leaf. Would the officers and the physician come before the thief might revive and escape? She felt too weak to try overpowering him a second time.

The worried girl became aware that the kitchen door was opening. From where she sat Bess saw Fred Jenkins enter. "I must do something fast to keep him from finding out!" Bess thought.

The only thing left to her was conversation. Mustering all the courage she possessed, Bess hurried to the kitchen and smiled broadly at Fred. "I guess you're surprised to see me here," she said.

Fred looked scared. "Y-yes I am," he stuttered. "I thought you girls were going to be out for the afternoon."

Bess giggled. "You know how girls are. I got a good distance from here and then I remembered I'd forgotten something. Had to come back and get it. Then I decided to use the phone." Bess smiled. "Do you have a steady girl friend?"

"Why n-no," Fred answered. He kept glancing around and looking very uncomfortable. Finally he said, "Are you alone?"

Bess laughed. "What do you think I am—three people? Maybe I'm heavy enough to make three, but I do try to diet. Fred, how do you manage to stay so slim?"

"Me? I don't know. Did anyone come into the house after you did?"

Bess answered lightly, "Oh, I know Mr Rorick and Mrs Holman won't be back for some time. As for Nancy and George, I'll be joining them in a few minutes. As soon as I've talked to you a little longer.

"Tell me, Fred, do you like having odd jobs at different places? Wouldn't you rather have a steady job somewhere?" Before he had a chance to answer, she went on, "You know, if you plan to get married some-time, your wife would want you to have a full-time job."

Fred frowned. "I like what I'm doing. How soon are you leaving?"

Bess shrugged. "You sound as if you want to get rid of me. Don't you like talking to me?"

"Why—er—yes," Fred replied.

Bess kept listening eagerly for the sound of the police car. She wondered how much longer she could keep Fred in the kitchen talking about inconsequential matters. She struggled on bravely. "Wouldn't you like a snack?" She opened the refrigerator door. "Umm, I see some delicious pudding. Want some?"

"No."

"How about a piece of cake?" Bess moved over to the cakebox.

"No."

As he said this, a feeling of relief came over Bess. She had heard a car roar up to the front of the house. "That must be friends of mine," she told Fred. "I'll be seeing you!"

As he stood rooted to the spot, she dashed to the front door and opened it. Chief Rankin, two other officers, and a physician hurried in. Quickly she said, "Go and get that young man who's just running out the kitchen door!"

Two of the officers raced in and captured the escapee.

As he was led back into the kitchen, Fred glared at Bess. "You! You double-crossed me!"

"Yes, I did. Your father—or whoever that man is you pal around with—is lying in the library unconscious."

"What!" Fred cried out. "My father is hurt!"

"So he is your father," said Bess. To the police she directed, "Follow me!"

She led the group into the dining-room and showed them the open door and the secret passage-way to the library. Having been in the house several times before, the officers stared at it, astounded.

Fred Jenkins' eyes almost popped **out** of his head. "You found it!"

"Nancy Drew found it," Bess answered. "She and my cousin George are lying in that room unconscious. Your father used a knockout spray gun on them!"

"You said my father was unconscious too," said Fred. "What happened to him?" When Bess told him, the young man blinked. "You're—you're that brave?"

Bess did not reply. Instead, she suggested that the group hurry through the passageway into the library. She herself would go to Nancy's room for the key to the new padlock. When she returned and opened it, the alarm sounded. Bess inquired of the physician how Nancy and George were.

"They'll come round in a few minutes," he answered. "No harmful after-effects. As to Mr Jenkins, he got a nasty bruise on his head as he fell. He'll take a while to wake up."

As the doctor finished speaking, Nancy stirred and opened her eyes. George took a few moments longer. Both girls blinked and looked from face to face. They were amazed to see the police, and stared up at Fred Jenkins, then across the floor towards his father.

Nancy sat up and asked what had happened. She and

George were assisted to chairs and then Bess told her story.

Both girls looked at her in utter astonishment. "Bess, our timid one!" said George.

Bess merely smiled. Suddenly her legs were getting rubbery. She was feeling the emotional strain and flopped on to the couch.

"I think Fred can clear up many points of the mystery," Bess said.

With a bit of braggadocio, the young man admitted that he had discovered the openings to the secret passageway. One day, while cleaning the dining-room, he had caught the faint glint of metal between two of the panels above the mantelshelf. He had picked at it with a knife, and suddenly the door had opened. The rest was easy.

"My father," he went on, "has two friends who know a lot about the sinking of the *Lucy Belle*. They think a treasure was taken from the wreck and buried somewhere around here. They went to the public library and the one at the university for some books that might tell about it but learned nothing."

Nancy said, "They must be the men Ned heard talking one day."

"They helped us trail you girls wherever you went. John Tregger and Hank More are smart. Oh, I shouldn't have mentioned their names." The police had already made notes. Nancy was sure the men would be picked up for questioning.

Fred shrugged and went on, "The four of us began to hunt and dig, but we didn't have any luck. Then after I found the secret way to get into the library, and saw all those books, my father said he would look through them. He was sure there must be some old records which would give him a hint. While he worked, I stood guard."

Nancy spoke up. "If you were trying to keep this thing so secret, why did you use light in the woods?"

Fred grinned. "That was my idea. After my father got into the locked room and disturbed the books, I heard Mrs Holman say nobody but a phantom could get into it. I thought I'd make the whole thing spooky and scare people off while we were digging. By the way, we always covered the places over with leaves, so you wouldn't find them!"

"What about the money you stole?" Nancy asked.

Fred looked blank. "I don't know anything about any money, honest. You mean money taken from this room?"

"Yes, plenty of it."

All this time the doctor had been working on Mr Jenkins and now the thief regained consciousness. When he was assisted to a chair, Chief Rankin said, "As soon as you feel able, *talk*."

The man looked sullenly from face to face, but glared at Nancy, George, and Bess. At first he was silent, but after a few prodding questions from Nancy, he admitted his guilt.

"I used to be a locksmith by trade," he said, "and also an expert on opening safes."

He admitted that the outfit at the river cabin was his. He had made keys to the various doors and padlocks in the Rorick home.

"If you could open the padlocks, why did you bother with the passageway?" George asked.

"So I wouldn't get caught. I was hiding in the passageway several times while other people were in the room."

Chief Rankin asked Jenkins why he had waited so long before robbing the safe. The man said he had found the combination a very tricky and difficult one to figure out.

"Tell me," said Nancy, "did you take only small amounts of money at a time from the books to avoid suspicion?"

Jenkins gave a wise smile. "I knew that Mr Rorick probably wouldn't notice. A tenner here and there kept me supplied with all I needed."

Fred stared at his father in shocked surprise. "What else did you take?" he asked.

Jenkins grinned at his son and confessed to the theft of the coins. He said those still missing were hidden in the guest house.

He also admitted having tried to frighten Nancy away from the Rorick home. When he found out the owner had asked her to solve the mystery, he had coaxed his two friends to help him scare her away. One had swamped Nancy and Ned's canoe, the other had shrieked in the woods when Ned was in the Indian costume, "We hoped these things would get you off our trail," he told Nancy, "but I guess you don't scare easy."

"Did you steal my pearl necklace?" she asked.

"Yes. It's hidden in the cabin. You look under the floor boards. Why do I want to give it back to you? Because I admire your grit!"

This was the first time in Nancy's life that a thief had voluntarily offered to return property because he admired her! She had to smile.

During the next fifteen minutes Fred Jenkins and his father made several other admissions. Fred's father had thought of the prank of the thumbprints. He knew a very large man with huge thumbs and for a fee got him to make marks on several papers.

"I sure had you fooled that time I dropped one of the papers." He smirked. "I was up in a tree all the time but you never spotted me."

Fred admitted to pretending that there had been a phone call for Nancy about Hannah Gruen, and pushing the threatening note under the front door. He had taken Nancy's car away to wash it. His father had helped him start the motor without a key. They had taken the car to the shack along the river. While Fred washed it, his father had made a key to the ignition to make it easier to drive back.

"We didn't leave the key in the lock, but I said it had been there to make you think the phantom had done it and you'd worry."

"What I want to know," said Nancy, "is whether or not you found any part of the treasure from the *Lucy Belle*."

Mr Jenkins shook his head. "If it's true that the treasure is still around, it's well hidden."

Chief Rankin interrupted. "If you girls have no further questions to do with the robbery, we'll take these two men in. Please ask Mr Rorick to come down to headquarters and make a formal charge against them."

The prisoners were led away. Bess said, "Won't Uncle John and Mrs Holman be amazed when they return? Just think, the mystery is solved!"

Nancy corrected her. "Only one of Uncle John's two mysteries. Don't forget we haven't found the wedding gifts."

George said she did not have one single hunch to offer Nancy. Bess declared her brain would not work any more.

"Well, I have an idea," said Nancy. "Suppose that the Indians were kind to the exhausted survivors and helped the thieving crewmen bury the treasure, thinking it belonged to everyone. In return, the crewmen promised the Indians a share of it, but did not intend to keep the promise. When they sneaked back later to dig it up, the Indians, upon discovering they had been double-crossed, became furious at all the survivors and killed them.

"The old map shows that the massacre took place near the village. I'll bet that's where we'll find the pine tree landmark Ned thought he had located on the shore."

George stood up. "It's a long chance, but let's go!"

"Now?" Bess asked.

"Right now."

Once more the girls got their digging tools and set off for the site of the Indian village. They found no old pine trees, but after a short search they located a huge, old stump.

"Let's start here," Nancy proposed.

As Bess shoved a spade into the ground, she remarked, "Nancy Drew, you'd better be right this time, because this is the last digging I'm going to do!"

Nancy and George laughed as they took positions and began to work. The ground was hard from lack of rain and the job was not easy. The girls kept on, however.

They had almost completed a deep circle around the stump, when suddenly George exclaimed that her spade had hit something. The other two girls began to help her dig away the earth. In ten minutes two iron chests were uncovered, one on top of the other. After crusted dirt had been brushed off, the words *Lucy Belle* could be seen on the lid of the top chest.

"We've found it!" George exclaimed.

The chest was locked and it took a lot of prying with a spade to lift the lid. The girls' eyes bulged at the contents—a huge heap of gold coins!

"There must be millions of them!" Bess cried out.

"What a haul!" said George.

"But not for us," Nancy reminded them. "I suppose this belongs to the town of Emerson."

At her suggestion, the three friends combined their strength to lift the heavy chest out of the hole. Then Nancy brushed the earth off the one below it. The name Rorick stood out in bold lettering cut into the metal. Eagerly the girls hauled the second chest to the surface. In it they found a small leather trunk with a curved top. On this the name Abigail Rorick had been painted.

"The gifts!" Bess said in a hushed voice.

"Uncle John has the key to it!" Nancy exclaimed.

George said practically, "How are we ever going to get these things to the Rorick house? They're too heavy to carry."

For a few minutes no one could answer her question. Nancy glanced around at the trees. "Maybe we could make a carry-all of poles like the Indians used to do."

At her direction, the three digging tools were laid a few feet apart. Next, the girls gathered blown-down saplings, which they stripped of branches and placed side by side across the metal part of the spades.

"Won't we have to tie the chests on to the poles?" Bess asked.

Nancy said she did not think so if the girls held the handles of the spades close to the ground as they dragged them along.

It was hard work, but slowly the trio pulled their precious cargo through the woods and up to the Rorick back lawn. Just as they arrived at the rose garden, Mrs Holman glanced from the kitchen window. A minute later she and Uncle John hurried out, astonished.

"What on earth—?" the housekeeper began.

For answer, Nancy slipped open the chest of coins. "And you have the key to the little trunk, Uncle John."

"I can't believe my eyes!" he cried out. "Where? How?"

The utter bewilderment on the faces of the two older people almost amused Nancy. "We'll carry these inside while you get the key, Uncle John."

He went for it and inserted the dainty key into the corroded lock, and after much difficulty, finally turned it. As the girls pushed back the lid, everyone gasped in admiration.

Neatly packed was one of the most exquisite wedding dresses they had ever seen. With it were very pointed high-heeled white satin slippers, now yellowed with age.

The lovely veil looked so fragile that the girls were afraid to touch it, but they did pick up the ivory-handled, hand-painted fan which had been the French queen's gift to Abigail Rorick.

"It's beautiful!" Nancy exclaimed.

At the bottom of the chest lay a velvet jewel case. Uncle John asked Nancy to open it. Within, pinned to the satin lining of the case, were two exquisite miniatures painted on ivory. They were framed with jewels.

"How gorgeous! They're portraits of Louis Phillipe and his queen!" she exclaimed.

Everyone continued to stare at the array of beauty for several minutes. Then finally George said, "Wait until you hear the rest of what happened while you were away."

When she finished, Uncle John and his housekeeper were open-mouthed with amazement.

"Treasures! Gifts! The phantom in jail! A secret passageway uncovered!" Mr Rorick exclaimed. He added, "I can never thank you girls enough. What can I do to show my appreciation?"

Nancy laughed. "Don't forget that you took us in when we were homeless. That was a very big favour."

Uncle John declared that the solving of the two mysteries was cause for a celebration. "We'll have it right here. I'll engage caterers to serve the food. Among the guests will be people from the university and officials of the town of Emerson."

"And Mrs Palmer," put in Nancy. "I promised to tell her the outcome of the mystery."

"Certainly," said Uncle John. "Then together you girls and I will present the chest of gold coins to the town officials and the wedding gown and other pieces to the university museum." Suddenly he grinned. "But not these precious miniatures. These I will keep and give to the first of you three girls to be married!"

Nancy, Bess, and George blushed and Nancy quickly changed the subject by saying she wondered what her next mystery would be. It was not long before she became involved in *The Mystery of the Fire Dragon.*

"Perhaps the museum would like the piece of ribbon we found in the Indian cave," Nancy suggested.

A strange look came over the old man's face. "You —you found that place!" he exclaimed. "Why, I could have told you all about it and the ribbon, too. I used to play there as a boy. Why didn't you tell me?" he added.

"I thought I did," said Nancy, and was sure she had. "But," she added politely, "I'm afraid I forgot. I'm sorry."

The old man chuckled. "Think nothing of it, my dear," he said. "All of us forget things now and then— even," he added, patting her hand, "the best of young lady detectives!"